"Get out of my home, Dominic Catalano!"

Letitia had read about white-hot rage—she had never thought to experience it. She went on between clenched teeth, "How I ever thought you could even be a friend is beyond me...."

"Oh, no, not a friend," He smiled down at her with thinned lips. "Oh, no," he repeated, "there's no friendship involved now. Now I'm going to make love to you. Make love in my own fashion, completely. You can think of Madison afterwards, but I can guarantee that for a time you'll forget him."

Beginning to be frightened in earnest, Letitia tried to tell him why Peter had been here, but his lips came down on hers.

He was kissing her now, deep, slow, heartbreaking kisses. She wasn't going to respond...she wasn't. She was far too angry.

Mons Daveson remembers sending off her first manuscript after a great deal of work—only to have it rejected. She is now, however, a seasoned author who appreciates the pleasures and frustrations that come with writing. ''There is a certain feeling you get when you start a story,'' she explains, ''a story that has been building, little by little, segment by segment, within the mind, and see the actual words written down.'' It is a feeling of satisfaction once all the sentences and paragraphs finally come together. Mons grew up in the ruggedly beautiful Australian outback, has visited all parts of her country and now lives with her family in Brisbane.

Books by Mons Daveson

HARLEQUIN ROMANCE

    1—PROMISE ME
   19—OUT OF THE BLUE
1415—THE HOUSE IN THE FOOTHILLS
1456—THIS TOO I'LL REMEMBER
2461—LAND OF TOMORROW
2534—MY LORD KASSEEM
2575—MACKENZIE COUNTRY
2756—GIRL OF MYSTERY

Don't miss any of our special offers. Write to us at the following address for information on our newest releases.

Harlequin Reader Service
901 Fuhrmann Blvd., P.O. Box 1397, Buffalo, NY 14240
Canadian address: P.O. Box 603,
Fort Erie, Ont. L2A 5X3

No Gentle Encounters

Mons Daveson

Harlequin Books

TORONTO • NEW YORK • LONDON
AMSTERDAM • PARIS • SYDNEY • HAMBURG
STOCKHOLM • ATHENS • TOKYO • MILAN

Original hardcover edition published in 1989
by Mills & Boon Limited

ISBN 0-373-17053-X

Harlequin Romance first edition January 1990

CHAPTER ONE

'MISS FORREST!' The voice emanating from the man who had just come to stand before her was clipped, concise, and assured, she thought. She found herself looking at a complete stranger; a tall stranger, clad in navy linen.

And, turning away from her lawyer, who was telling her, 'I'll see you on Monday, Letitia,' as he gently patted her shoulder before walking off, she went to speak the conventional words of greeting to this new individual.

They ended in almost a gasp, as she found herself gazing into eyes holding the vividness of emeralds; into the glinting, sparkling shine of deep, deep green. Elongated, slanting, their shape compelled attention as well as that startling colour which leaped out from the tanned, handsome face.

She must have answered his condolences—she couldn't remember! Her hand was freed, and she put it, tingling, behind her back like a little girl.

The man was speaking to her brother now, casual words about tobacco, she thought. And then he had disappeared among the thinning groups.

Heavens! The ejaculation was only a thought in the girl's mind as she stood motionless beside the open door of their car. Johnny had spoken as if he knew this man, but she had never met him before. He was one person anyone would remember.

That aquiline face, that tall lithe body, from broad shoulders to lean tapering hips, could have come from the mould of a Roman god of old. For he was an

Italian. His skin showed a deeper brown from the ordinary bronzed sheen endemic to the far north with its brilliant, blazing sunshine. It was not merely a tan; it owed its origin to the south of Europe, Letitia suspected.

Even as she tried to dismiss this stranger from her mind, she was seeing those eyes again. Those magnetic eyes. No one would forget them, even though cool uninterest had been the only expression they had held.

Getting into the car to depart, she said absently to her brother as she always did, 'Drive carefully.' He only held a learner's licence. Then she bent to lay her head on her arm resting on the window.

But Johnny wasn't speaking absently as he turned to her. He said firmly, 'You mustn't be sad, Sis. Grandfather wouldn't have wanted you to be—you know he told us both so.'

'Yes, I know! And I suppose we shall have to start making plans—without him in them . . . Oh, well.'

They drove towards the small town of Mareeba, through and out the other side, and beneath narrowed eyelids Letitia watched the familiar scene outside their swiftly moving car slide past. For it was familiar. She had lived here all her life—all twenty years of it.

She felt a hand come to rest on her thigh; to give her comfort, she suspected. She sat up straight and smiled across at this young brother of hers. He smiled back, relieved, and returned to his driving.

But suddenly she was gazing more intently, more assessingly, at the farm they were passing, fenced, painted, and immaculate, the tobacco crop invisible from the road. But the acre upon acre of shining green coffee plants was not. They stretched into the distance. And through them, and past a screen of trees, came a glimpse of the long white villa that was the Catalano home. The house belonging to that man she had just met—Dominic Catalano.

It had slid away, and then they were past the next two farms before turning into their driveway. Descending from the car, Letitia suddenly felt all her energy draining away, and, moving out back to the veranda, she sank into a low cane chair.

'Stay there, Sis. I'll get us some tea,' said Johnny.

Leaning back, she raised a hand to push the hair carelessly away from her face. She didn't know how fragile and vulnerable she looked, with her clear grey eyes and the fair, silver-gilt, almost ash-blonde hair. But she wasn't fragile; she was tall for a girl at just on five foot five, and she was strong and supple from the outdoor life she led. But she was not beautiful. However, her apricot-tanned skin, which she always protected from the burning sun up here, accompanied by that eye-catching hair, made her stand out in a crowd.

The wide grey eyes came open as her brother returned with a laden tray. Smiling lovingly at him, she said, 'Thank you, handsome.'

Depositing the tea equipage upon a white-enamelled table, Johnny poured the hot, strong brew, and passed a cup across. He said, 'I think you'd better find another nickname for me after this afternoon.'

Puzzled, she asked, 'This afternoon?'

'Too right! After meeting that Catalano bloke! Isn't he the handsomest hunk of male you've ever seen?'

'I don't know about that, Johnny. I didn't see very much of him.' Letitia shut her mind to the shock her whole metabolism had received when she had met those extraordinary eyes. 'I wasn't taking much notice of people this afternoon.'

'Well, take my word for it, he is! And even if it was only from politeness when he said that if there was anything he could help me with, feel free to ask, he's going to find he has a surprise coming: I intend to do just that. His farm grows the best tobacco in the district and as I'm putting in a crop this year, I'll certainly be going there for all the advice I can get.'

'Look, I know Catalano owns that big property just down from us, but how do you know him, Johnny? I'm sure I've never seen him before.'

'Oh, I met him once at the courts some time ago, when he stopped there for a few minutes to drop young Vanni off. The word around is that he's come home to stay. That he's left the south and big business, and come home to grow coffee and tobacco.'

'Still, you know how to grow tobacco, Johnny. We've grown it all our lives . . . until Grandfather couldn't manage.'

'Yes, OK, I realise that. But I was only a kid then . . . and you know how the world progresses, and times and methods change.'

'You really aren't going back to school, then?' Letitia asked the question and wanted an answer, but her glance was following a flock of galahs as they flew overhead in a vivid cloud of lollipop-pink.

'Don't be silly, Sis. What for? I've got all the education I need. And the farm is where I'm going to live my life. A farmer's all I want to be!'

Her attention returned from a sky suddenly devoid of birds to this loved seventeen-year-old brother of hers. And, whatever he had said about that man she had met today, he was a handsome boy. So, 'OK then,' she answered, 'plant a crop this year. But you do have Peter to show you all you need to know. He, or someone like him, probably showed this Catalano man how. That's Peter's job.'

'Fat chance of that! Knowing this Dominic bloke, I bet he knew everything about everything before he started. But about Peter . . .'

Her brother broke off to refill his cup, then he began to speak slowly as if searching for words. 'You've played tennis and partnered him away at young farmers' outings. Are you going to marry him?' The question came somewhat anxiously.

Was she? Letitia didn't think so. She knew she had occasionally played around with the idea, because Peter had been attentive, and he was quite attractive . . . but that was all it had been, playing around with an idea.

She said now, carefully, 'Oh, I don't think so, and it's manners to wait until you're asked. But for now, I've got to get a new life started for myself, so I'll be off to town to start looking for a job. And don't you forget, if I have to be away all day, you take good care of my mango trees.'

'Oh, come on Sis! There's no need for you to go working somewhere else . . . we'll manage here very well.'

'Yes, I expect we could . . . however, we'll leave all that until after the weekend, and on Monday talk business, and see banks. Right?'

She smiled across at him and added, 'I'm going to have a shower now—and what's that phrase they use in books and films—get into something more comfortable.'

Pushing back her chair, she went through the long room that ran the length of the house, kitchen at one end, living-room at the other, her dark grey dress swinging beneath her knees. Showering, she allowed the streaming water to wash away memories of the past hours, then dried, and in her bedroom, she stepped deliberately into pink shorts and a pink T-shirt. Start as you mean to go on, her grandfather would be telling her. And she was going to make laughter and happiness the theme song of this place from now on.

So, pushing back the silver-gilt hair and tying it high at the back in a ponytail, she heard the shower going again, and murmured, 'Good, Johnny's getting into more suitable clothes too.' But when she had finished dressing, she waited a moment to look at herself. Looking for good points—and bad ones; knowing, though not acknowledging it, why she was doing so.

She found her grey eyes suddenly gazing deep into eyes of gleaming emerald; the cold gleam of that jewel, she reflected acidly, remembering . . . Oh, well, everyone couldn't be handsome like Roman gods. And her figure wasn't too bad, with those long apricot tanned legs. She shrugged slim shoulders at the reflection, and left.

On the back veranda, meaning to clear away the tea tray, she saw that it had already been done, and her young brother was leaning against the railing. The shorts and T-shirt he wore, however, were white. He turned as she came towards him and, grinning, gave a long imitation of a wolf-whistle.

Letitia grinned back, saying, 'Just don't I wish I collected those whenever I make an appearance! Look, Johnny, come for a walk with me among the mango trees. They soothe me.'

Around the back from the veranda they walked to where some distance away was the green smudge that was the mango orchard. 'I'm so glad I persuaded Grandfather to put them in,' she said. Who knows how long tobacco will be grown, with so many voices crying out against it . . .'

Interrupting, her brother said, 'Yes, I know. And I accept some of what's being said. But look at all the other, much nastier things in the world. They'll have to start dealing with them as well. Everything in moderation is my motto.'

Astonished, Letitia started laughing and couldn't stop. The words he had uttered were so unlike this casual brother of hers. What had he and his friends talked about at school? She would have bet everything that their conversation had been about tennis, school work when it had to be . . . and, oh yes, girls!

She gazed up at him, but all he had to add was, 'I'll race you to the first trees . . . and I'll beat you, I bet!' He let go of her arm and was off. Willy-nilly, she followed that flying figure, endeavouring to overtake it.

Johnny was hanging on to the trunk of one of the small trees when she caught up with him, and together, arm in arm, they strolled through the little forest, the girl gazing complacently at the dark green, thick foliage. Common mangoes were fruit she had grown up with all her life. But these were different. Bowen Specials, able to be sliced with a knife, they brought a fortune down south.

And now, walking among the green shelter of these trees which her grandfather had helped her plant, suddenly flashing into her mind came words she had once spoken to him at some mention of his lost only son. 'Never mind,' she had told him, swinging on his arm. 'When I grow up and get married, I'll have six children for you. So there!'

He had lifted her up in his arms, laughing. And through all the different strands with which their lives had been warped, his was the one that showed clear and shining. But now, on this lovely evening, with a crimson sun sliding on its way to bed for the night, with the deep azure arch above turning to a delicate shade of eggshell blue, Letitia knew that that part of her life had gone. Tomorrow was the start of a new one.

Interrupting her reverie, Johnny's voice said, 'Peter's just driven up. I thought he'd probably come.' So they turned, walking to meet the vehicle as it pulled up half-way along the drive, its official Primary Industry Department logo showing through the dusk of its exterior.

'Hi,' said Johnny to the young man stepping from the vehicle. 'I'm off to have an assessing look at my barns,

Peter. I'll see you.'

Their visitor walked across and reaching out his hands took both of Letitia's into them. 'What do I say? It's hard to know.'

Smiling, she went to free his grip, and found it too tight. 'There's nothing for you to say, Peter. It's over! See, I've just been looking at my mangoes. Aren't they in good shape?'

However, the young man before her wasn't interested in trees. His brown face, under waving brown hair, was gazing directly into hers, and a vagrant thought flashed abruptly through her mind that it was not half as dark as another face into which she had looked this afternoon, and the brown eyes weren't a startling vivid green either.

She shook her head to clear it, her attention returning with a rush as she took in what he was saying. 'You know how I feel, Letitia. I couldn't really say much before. But we've danced together at the Club. We've played tennis together, although,' with a wide smile, 'I acknowledge that you're better at it than I am. But you know, I think we'll hit it off very well together . . .'

Before he could go on, she broke in, 'Yes, we've had some good times, Peter. But look, I don't feel like discussing anything just now. Please leave things for the moment. Also, your term of duty up here is almost up, isn't it? And I have Johnny to think of. He's all the family I have now, you know.'

'Of course you have your brother to think of.' The words carried amusement. 'But he'll have his own life. And we can be engaged for the few months or so of my stay here—until he's settled.'

'No! We really will leave it, Peter. I don't feel like talking about anything at all now.'

'OK! I should have waited. But,' his glance moved over the slim, tall young figure, clad in minute pink shorts, 'you look so fetching, I had to say something.'

Letitia smiled back at him. They had got on very well, in a casual way, but she would have to think very carefully about what he was proposing.

Peter took her arm as they turned to stroll down the driveway. They sat on the back veranda and watched red streaks of a violent sunset gild the tea-trees growing in the centre channel of the river. It was a magical time of evening—birds flying home, the whisper of branches above swaying in the night-coming breeze.

She glanced suddenly around, aware of Peter's gaze upon her. He said, 'I can understand how you feel just now, Letitia, but . . .'

Moving across to her, he reached down to pull her to her feet and into his arms. She knew he meant to kiss her, so she laughed softly into his face, saying as she turned her head, 'Really, Peter!' And over his shoulder, her eyes looked blankly at the two figures rounding the side of the veranda; at the expression showing on the face of one . . . the tall one.

She pulled violently, and found herself sharply released as Peter heard Johnny's voice. He swung round and said quite happily as if he didn't mind being caught in the position he had been in, 'Hi there, Dominic, you're straying from your own bailiwick, aren't you?'

'I have someone coming over on Sunday night whom I thought Johnny might like to meet . . . and, of course, Miss Forrest.'

The smooth, clipped words brought the colour flying to Letitia's cheeks. But it was the contemptuous expression in those vividly green eyes that deepened the rose-pink to a crimson red.

How dared he gaze at her like that, she thought, as if she were some . . . some . . .? Arrogance wasn't the word for the way his glance was moving over her!

Her colour turned even deeper as those extraordinary eyes continued, looking her over from head to toe . . .

moving more slowly down the long, tanned legs, when his glance reached them, then up again across the diminutive pink shorts and top.

What did he know of the reason that had made her dress like this, on this day? Letitia went to speak through clenched teeth, wishing she lived in a society that would approve of her slapping that expression from the assessing arrogant face. But before she could get the words out, Peter said, 'I've come to offer my condolences. I thought doing it privately would be best.'

'So I see,' said the Catalano man.

Yes, he had seen, thought Letitia, and he was now using words as well as glances to put his judgement across.

And to say those three sarcastic words to Peter too! It was Peter's job to know all the farmers, and their farms. Because he was here to give advice. But of course that man standing there in front of her, still busy looking her over, would never need advice! she thought wrathfully.

Johnny was glancing from one to another, puzzled by an atmosphere that hung around their four figures like a cloud of electricity. He knew Peter well, he had found Mr Catalano pleasant and helpful. He said, suddenly breaking into the small silence that had fallen, 'It's too late for tea, but would you like a drink?' He smiled his happy smile at all three of them before continuing. 'I'm afraid it will be only beer—or orange juice. I know you drink beer, Peter. What about you, Mr Catalano? I also know Italians drink wine a lot, but we haven't any, I'm sorry.'

'Beer will be fine, Johnny. And yes, I would like a drink.' Their visitor moved easily up on to the veranda with the words, and half sat, half lounged on the railings, friendliness issuing from him as far as Johnny was concerned.

Letitia moved back and sank thankfully into the chair

from which she had just been pulled. She found her legs were shaking. Let Johnny get the drinks, she decided. She wasn't going to play hostess to this man. Not after the way he had looked—and spoken—to her.

What business of his was it if she chose to wear pink this afternoon? He didn't belong in her life. But of course, being an Italian, he probably thought she should be dressed in deepest black, she raged inwardly. Well, he could go jump. He knew nothing of the situation!

Johnny arrived with the drinks and, seeing them, for the first time in the past few minutes Letitia allowed herself a natural smile. Meeting her satirical glance, her young brother's face now carried a tinge of red.

The glasses he was handing round so carefully were the crystal goblets that had been passed down from their grandmother. They were seldom used.

Apparently her brother didn't dislike this visitor who had so unexpectedly entered their life today.

They drank their drinks; the men talked growing tobacco and its hazards, her brother putting in his own pennyworth. Letitia sat silent, swishing her ice round in the dregs of her orange juice.

From under downcast lashes, she looked at that man leaning so carelessly on the veranda railings, and thought that he couldn't talk, or look either! Because he had also changed. He wore casual fawn cords with pockets slashed in the front below the waistline, and a pale lemon shirt—much more see-through than anything she was wearing, she told herself indignantly. With no undershirt on, one could see the muscles on the broad brown chest rippling beneath it when he moved. Probably handmade to measure to show them off, she reflected sarcastically, her lips curling a little.

He wore no jewellery, not even a signet ring; only a thin gold watch on a leather strap. And as her gaze rested on that elegant timepiece, the hand wearing it rose, her glance doing the same just as quickly. The Catalano man emptied his glass and shook his head at her brother, who had made a move to refill it, saying,

'No, thank you, Johnny, I have to leave—but first——' he looked impartially between the young boy and the girl sitting in her chair, then said, 'The word has been going around that you intend putting in a crop this year, Johnny. I know a man who'd be ideal for this place . . . of course you'd have to check him out with your advisers, but I couldn't recommend him too highly.'

Before the boy could reply, Letitia said swiftly, 'We really haven't decided what we're going to do yet, Mr Catalano. Thank you for your suggestion, but we wouldn't want to bother you!' Politely, socially, she smiled carefully across at him.

And those sculptured lips sent back a smile holding exactly the same content. 'Oh, it would be no bother,' he told her.

Johnny broke in quickly, 'Oh, yes, Letitia, I'd like to meet the man. Could we, Mr Catalano? Because of course I'll have to have someone.'

What could she say? She stood there, hating this tall man and everything about him. Why had she ever had to meet him? Why had he ever come here to her home? And then she thought she should be ashamed. He had properly offered condolences. And this could be just a friendly offer to someone young and bereft from a man, experienced and wealthy, who lived near by.

That same man was continuing, 'He'll be at a barbecue I'm giving on Sunday evening. If you'd like to come, I'll see you around six o'clock. So long until then. I'll be off.' He waved to all three of them and turned to go.

Letitia rose too. She said, 'I'll see you both off. We're going to have an early night.'

Perforce, Peter had to rise too, and the four of them walked round the veranda to the far side. Letitia caught Johnny's arm as he went to go further, and they stood, the fair brother and sister, silhouetted in the last of the evening light.

But the female of the duo was saying to herself, I really don't want to go to that man's place. I feel I don't want to go anywhere near him. But she knew she would have to. For Johnny's sake, what else could she do?

CHAPTER TWO

HER GAZE on the familiar countryside sliding past, Letitia said, 'You know I didn't really want to come, Johnny. We've lived near these people for always and I've probably only nodded as we met. As for the owner of it all, I've never seen him before. Oh, I do wish I was back home!' The last sentence came out almost angrily.

'Come on, Letitia! You've never gone anywhere much before where you could meet anyone, because Grandfather was so unwell. You only went to the Tennis Club and their "do"s. But things can change now. And Dominic Catalano needn't have gone to the trouble he has just to help me.

'Because as well as his enormous tobacco acreage, he's a business man too. And just look at his coffee! Tobacco's the money-spinner up here, but everyone is beginning to diversify. Only look at our beautiful mangoes—they should be producing soon, you know. Who knows, we might be famous ourselves one day, with holdings as big as the Catalano ones. Just give me time!'

Her brother laughed, and Letitia joined in. There was no way that could happen, but still, they could have a laugh about it, and hadn't she only now vowed that their place was going to be a happy home?

She would go to this party—and she would make herself enjoy it. There wouldn't be just Dominic Catalano there.

But absently, thinking of what Johnny had said, Letitia remarked, 'He probably has got tons of money, with that enormous farm of his. And he doesn't work it

18

himself; he has a manager and men to do that.'

Johnny's wide grin flashed in reply. 'Yes, I can imagine you could be right about that! Here we are.' He swung off the road to where they were stopped by a big closed gate. A young boy sitting on the fence beside it jumped down to swing it wide.

'Hi there, Vanni,' greeted Johnny. 'How's it going? Do you think you can beat me at tennis yet?'

'Oh, maybe not yet,' he was answered with a laugh. 'But I'm working on it.'

Johnny laughed too as he eased the car through the opening as it was shut behind them.

'Heavens! We could be back in old-world Europe. Peasants to open the gates, no less!' As soon as the words came out, Letitia wondered at herself. It must be just the thought of that arrogant man and the forced acceptance of this invitation that had put her nerves on edge, she surmised.

Johnny had turned a surprised stare at her. 'That's young Giovanni. His father is the manager of this outfit, and,' an arm went out in a throwaway gesture, 'he's a junior at the Tennis Club.'

Her brother seldom spoke to her in that tone, and she laid a placating hand on his knee. 'Sorry, Johnny,' she replied. 'I'm just being hard to get on with . . .'

'Sis——' the young boy paused after the one word, then resumed carefully, 'I do need to make a good job of planting this year, and to take all the expert advice I can get. That's the reason I accepted this invitation of Dominic Catalano's, OK?'

They were turning now into a circular gravelled driveway, pulling to a stop before a white-pillared veranda, and Letitia exclaimed for the second time this afternoon, thinking this place could have been a setting for *Gone with the Wind*. A man just emerging from the open doorway strolled to the edge of the steps.

Leaning out of his window, Johnny asked, 'Shall I

take this heap away somewhere, Mr Catalano?'

'No, just leave it and come along in.' A smile was sent impartially between the two of them.

They walked through a long, formal room, lounge on the one side, a heavily carved dining setting on the other, with a whole back wall of glass looking out on a vivid explosion of colour. It was only a glimpse as Letitia followed the man through a corner door into a large kitchen. Again all she got was an impression of colour, this time of gold, of lemon, from reflecting benches and tiled floor. Then they were out on to yet another tiled space—a veranda, from which echoed the sound of laughter and calling voices.

Here he stood aside, allowing her to precede him. Her elbow was grasped as he led her to a group who had turned as they emerged. It was only a light clasp in which Dominic held her, but unexpectedly, angrily telling herself she was imagining things, she felt the impression separately of every one of those long, tanned fingers. She heard him say, 'This is my cousin Joe,' and made herself sweep from her mind all thought of that firm hand she could still feel on the bare skin of her arm.

She received what was another small shock. 'My cousin Joe' to whom she managed to say a breathless hello, was blue-eyed and fair. And so was 'My cousin Ben'. She had been through so much lately, and this brilliantly lighted scene, these laughing, talking people, that clasp upon her, seemed to be making the whole setting something observed through a thin shining veil.

She met—always with that clasp upon her—people she already knew, and those she didn't. She met their lawyer, who said, 'Hi there, Letitia. See you tomorrow,' to which she only smiled. She remembered the food—a lot of it strange. And of course she remembered the dancing. She would always remember that dancing . . . with those strong fingers gripping her own instead of being firmly clasped about her elbow.

Then, thankfully, she found herself steered towards some youngsters at the far end of the veranda. She knew them enough to talk casually, and was grateful for the breathing space it allowed her.

She saw they were gathered on a tiled veranda running around three sides of the house, and from a courtyard of green lawn which it enclosed, a fountain was sending jets of crystal water high into a sky turning now to deep indigo. Darkness was taking over from the short twilight, easing them now into a warm, starlit tropical night.

Letitia stood sipping from a glass filled with ice and an unfamiliar fruit juice, when suddenly, feeling a gaze upon her, she glanced quickly around. She saw a glance studying her, completely focused, as if calculating other memories. But as she looked, the lids fell quickly over those eyes, allowing no sign of their thoughts to surface. A loud call came, and the owner of that puzzling gaze had swung away to answer.

He can't find fault with what I'm wearing this time, she decided a little angrily. For she had deliberately dressed for the occasion. She wore a white flared skirt, with a large frill of figured navy and white swirling at the hemline. Coupled with a light blue blouse finished off with old-fashioned coarse lace at collar and short puffed sleeves, it was inescapably right.

'It's a beautiful courtyard, isn't it?' she asked Joe, who was standing moodily beside her, and Ben laughed. Joe said, 'Yes, I think the whole house is beautiful. I built it! And if I can persuade my mother to get round Dominic, I'll build another one like it and make my name in Cairns. But I'm tired of this, we'll go and put some music on.'

'Will she?' asked Letitia curiously. She couldn't imagine anyone getting round that man if he didn't want to be got round. Ben laughed again.

Feeling her arm clasped for a second time that night, even if it was with different fingers that left no impression on either the arm or her metabolism, she went with Ben and another girl called Petra into the house.

Inside the big formal dining-room, Joe sent a large rug holding a carved table sliding along the polished tiles, saying, 'This will give us room,' and walked over to the hi-fi.

'You're not really going to dance on these, are you?' exclaimed Letitia, aghast, taking in the beautiful inlaid tiles she was standing on. She saw Ben reach for Petra's hand.

'Yes, we are going to dance on them, and we won't hurt them. I should know—I had them laid,' was all Joe answered.

Letitia shrugged. It was none of her business. The two younger ones were jiving, and then she found it *was* going to be her business. Joe said, 'Come along, Letitia.' He was holding out his hand.

But firmly she shook her head, telling him, 'I've never jived—I wouldn't know how to.'

'Everyone can jive, there's nothing to it,' was the answer she got back. 'Now, come on!' Both her hands were taken, and she was being shown how. She found quickly that you could make your own steps, so this she did in a small way, laughing across at her companion.

The music ended and she stood, cheeks flushed, breathing hard, and happier than she had been for a long time. Then the smile died on her face. The owner of this house was leaning indolently against a sofa and he was smiling at her; an ordinary, pleasant, 'glad you're enjoying yourself' smile.

And suddenly Letitia smiled back—at that tall figure dressed in pale green trousers that were made of doeskin, or leather, or some such stuff she had not seen before; in a pale green shirt like a lemon one she remembered . . . of so thin a material, it was almost see-through.

He said, 'Seeing you enjoyed that so much, Miss Letitia Forrest, you'd better try it again . . . with me.'

Her 'No!' echoed around the beautiful room.

'Oh, I think so,' he returned softly. 'Enjoyment is so nice to watch, it would be a pity not to continue with it.'

'But I can't imagine you dancing like that!' She hadn't meant to say that, it had just slipped out. Still, she really còuldn't.

His gaze swung to his cousin. He nodded. Joe turned to the hi-fi and the music began. Dominic added, 'And you two can go and help Rosa play host with the food while I'm busy.' He held out his hands, saying, 'Give me yours, Letitia.' And like a sleepwalker she put her own into the outstretched fingers.

Then, abruptly, there was no time to think of anything; she didn't even notice Johnny dancing with Petra. There was no one else but her partner, and those strong hands that caught and released hers as they twisted and turned together with feet sliding expertly over the tiles. There was only this entirely new sensation, these wild movements that took her completely out of herself.

It ended, as everything does in time, and Letitia stood immobile, looking up at him, cheeks coloured rose-pink, silver hair dishevelled, happiness a tangible element surrounding her. That wild dancing, the need to be a part of their two jiving bodies, had drawn her from her usual grave reserve into a wholly new dimension. She was also gazing directly into two eyes of vivid emerald green. Then the falling lids had dropped, hiding them. He said, 'We'd better go and see about food. Petra, Johnny!' They walked, the four of them, outside.

Two long tables had been set up on the green lawn of

the courtyard, and more people had arrived. Leaning back in her chair, Letitia shook her head in disbelief. This was a scene from out of glossy magazine advertisements. Something she had never been familiar with . . . a brilliant setting, blazing with a brightness that encircled the entire gathering. And some of the clothes! Again she shook her head.

She glanced opposite to where a small party was sitting on the steps of the other veranda, Johnny among them, plates on knees, forks busy.

A voice behind her said, 'Letitia,' and Petra was handing her a plate. 'My mother said you needed fattening up—her words, not mine!—so I think she's picked out something of everything for you.' The girl smiled down at her.

'And here's your wine,' put in 'my cousin Ben', whose name Letitia now knew was Peterson.

She smiled and took it, then put it on the floor by the railing. She ate slowly, joining in the party talk and laughter going on about her, finding unexpectedly that she was actually hungry, knowing she had not been hungry for quite some time. But from now on was another ball-game. Hadn't she vowed that?

From beneath downcast lashes she gazed around to see what the host of all this enjoyment was doing. She saw him sauntering among his guests, glass in hand. She glanced at the brilliant bed of flowers that showed each vivid petal illuminated, and wondered if it was from there that that haunting, elusive fragrance came. But it seemed to be wafting into here from beyond that grilled back opening. It wasn't honeysuckle or jasmine; she knew those.

A presence had materialised by her side to lean casually on the railings. 'Are you enjoying your meal, Letitia?' it asked. No 'Miss Forrest' tonight, she noticed.

He had stopped by her side, as he was doing by

everyone, she told herself as she answered carefully, 'Yes, I am, thank you. This seafood is delicious, but I'm afraid I can't cook exotic dishes. I do cook rather a mean roast, though . . .' She stopped abruptly, thinking, what a stupid thing to say!

But he was laughing, a soft laugh deep in his throat. 'Well, then,' he answered in that cool voice of his, 'you'll have to reciprocate, won't you? Your roast in exchange for my seafood and lasagne.'

Letitia thought, he's laughing at me, but then she saw his expression as his head turned and a gleam of light caught it. He wasn't laughing at her, she saw. And suddenly, between them, a line seemed to stretch—as thin as cotton, as tenuous as silken floss, but carrying the threaded strength of stretched steel.

She sat motionless, fork suspended. And the man, eyes wide open now, stayed immobile too, the wine in the glass his hand was holding still, unmoving.

Someone called, and in the hundredth part of a second Dominic moved, and quickly, breathlessly, endeavouring to bring another dimension into the charged atmosphere, Letitia asked, 'What's that perfume? It's lovely, and I've never been aware of it before.

The wine in his glass trembled and ran from one side of the crystal to the other as he drew a deep breath. But his tone was only amused, as he answered, 'Oh, that's Rosa's *dama de notte*. She brought it from the south with her, and I think it's a Mareeba trademark by now. I should imagine every second house or so up here has some of it. It does have a nice scent, doesn't it?'

'A nice scent? What sacrilege' Letitia spoke without thinking. 'It's exquisite. And if I can, I too am going to beg a piece to plant . . . right outside my bedroom window.'

Once again she was unable to see his expression, because only the merest glint showed between eyes

almost closed. Then at a shout of laughter from a group
of men and a call of 'Dominic!' he sketched a small
wave to them all, and strolled away.

She didn't know if it was Joe who was responsible,
but music was now a background to the whole party.
Some were dancing to the slow, romantic themes; but
Letitia only smiled and said she was still eating, when
someone asked her to join them. She had done all the
dancing she wanted to do for tonight.

She said to Joe, still leaning moodily on the railings a
few paces away, and she spoke oh, so casually, 'Your
cousin is rather a heartbreaker, isn't he?'

Her companion looked back along the veranda to
where Dominic was smiling down at a young woman
whose fingers were outspread upon that smooth brown
forearm.

'Oh, no,' was the quick reply, 'Dominic isn't a heartbreaker. My mother says he's the most straitlaced man
she knows. Oh, that doesn't mean . . .' Joe paused for a
moment, then continued, 'that he doesn't have his . . .
women friends. After all, look at who he is . . . and
what he has going for him!'

'Although now, just lately . . .' again came that
hesitant pause, 'we're all holding our breath. He's been
seen about with a girl in Cairns. They say she's beautiful; and she's very eligible. An Italian from that circle of
friends Dominic mixes with. Although with Dominic,'
Joe laughed suddenly with amusement, 'you can never
tell. He has a wide circle of friends—all from different
backgrounds.' He was abruptly gazing along to where
his cousin was still laughing down at that possessive
young woman, and his glance became more intent,
carrying speculation. 'You know,' he went on, 'such an
affair might soften him up, and I might get my way
with this place after all.'

His moodiness was seemingly dispelled, and he was
unexpectedly a charming and happy young man as he

strolled off.

The night progressed. People were beginning to leave, and glancing at her watch, Letitia was astonished to see it showing past eleven o'clock. She looked round for Johnny, wondering if he was pleased or satisfied with the man Dominic had taken him over to the manager's residence to see . . . before that wonderful, energetic dancing!

She hadn't mentioned it among all these people, in the atmosphere of enjoyment permeating the whole party. She would ask about it later.

Now she rose, and moving to the railing, called softly to her brother, who was dancing up and down the small cement path which connected the two verandas. He came to her and gave his wide smile.

'I think it's time to leave now, Johnny,' she told him. 'I don't want to be the last one to go.'

'Right,' he said at once. 'I'll just finish this.'

She waited while he finished the dance, then they made their way to Dominic, who smiled at them, saying, 'Off home? I'll see you out.' He brushed aside disclaiming words. So once again Letitia walked through the lovely formal rooms, this time without any guiding fingers on her arm, Dominic's tall figure still beside them as they moved down the front steps.

Lifting a fold of her full skirt away from a door about to close on it, he said, 'Until next time, Letitia. Goodnight!' Then he had turned away to go back to his other guests.

CHAPTER THREE

I DON'T believe it!' Letitia exclaimed.

'You'd better believe it. I wouldn't like it to get round that I can't draw up a simple will, or see to a transfer of money.'

'But . . .' Letitia gazed across at the lawyer. She said, smiling, 'Yes, I realise that, Mr Kamerson, but . . .'

'The thing is, my dear, the farm was left to your brother, the money to you, except for the income from the farm. And that Air Force pension of your father's has been mounting up over the years. You are now,' the lawyer smiled placidly at the young face looking at him, 'an heiress. However,' he waved a hand, 'only a minor one, you know. So my advice is to sit quietly on it for a while. All right?'

The lawyer began to gather up his papers; the interview was over. He did say as the two youngsters rose to leave, 'Oh, just for the record, what's the first thing you're going to buy?'

'I don't know . . .' Letitia hesitated, then her smile grew. 'Would one of those new trenching machines for my mangoes be in order?' Her smile had turned now into a grin. And the elderly man shook his head at them both—the girl and her brother. But all he got back was an affectionate wave before they turned laughingly to leave his office.

On the footpath outside, they stood among a hurrying crowd going about their own business. They also stood in a blue and golden day with scorching rays from a late summer's sun pouring down on them. These found and struck brilliant glints from silver-gilt hair swinging free on slim shoulders; they found, also, a gleam from clear grey eyes as they gazed laughingly into the youth's face opposite.

Two beautiful young people—the girl smiling up at the young man beside her as he spoke. Then, arm in arm, they turned, walking away.

They didn't see the man who had just emerged from an office block a few yards distant, and who had halted suddenly on catching sight of them. He remained immobile, suddenly transfixed, as his gaze fastened on the happy, smiling young girl, and abruptly, heavy lids fell over the vivid green beneath them until only a glinting look showed beneath slitted eyelids.

Then he had turned to walk quickly away, thrusting through people crowding the busy thoroughfare. In a side street, he unlocked the door of a long grey Jaguar, but once inside, he sat for a moment, quite still. Then he leaned over and turned a key. As the engine purred softly into life, the man swung the heavy vehicle around the corner and into the main street filled with traffic. He followed it until it branched out to open bushland.

The man and car passed, although he didn't see them, the same couple, who had just been served with tea. Letitia stirred the cube of sugar round and round in hers; she shook her head at the plate of pastries her brother passed across.

'No, I don't think so; but I think I do need this tea,' she told him, raising the cup to her lips.

'Are you maybe thinking of leaving here now, Letitia? You'll be able to now, with all that money.' A tinge of anxiety coloured Johnny's voice.

'As Mr Kamerson said, it's not all that much money! Anyway, I couldn't leave until you're eighteen. I'm your guardian, remember?' answered Letitia, laughing across at him. 'But your crop will be in by then, and by Christmas we'll know how you've done. I expect I could buy a farm for myself, and grow fruit, but . . .'

'Oh no, Sis, starting a farm from scratch would be too hard for you,' her brother interrupted quickly.

'Or . . .' his sister continued with a wry grin, 'I could go back to school, take my senior, then go on to university. How do you think I'd like Townsville?'

'I think you don't know what you want, so for now, off we'll go to the bank, then go and find something expensive to splurge on. And it won't be a trenching machine either!'

Letitia laughed, and answered, 'OK, but whatever I decide to do, a trenching machine will be an asset, and will make less work looking after my mango orchard. I'll get one, but not today.'

So they went—to the bank, to a hardware store, and to shop. But on the way back to the farm again, Letitia drew a deep thankful breath. She was happy to be going home. She might have been flying a few kites about doing other things, but really she knew that, with all its ups, and the down they had suffered, this town was where her heart was. It was all she knew, and she didn't want to go anywhere else to live.

She glanced back over her shoulder at the shopping they had splurged on, at the trenching machine brochures resting on the back seat—and smiled. 'Right OK, you mangoes, you'd better watch out!' she said. 'You're in for a big house-cleaning!'

Johnny laughed. And on reaching home, Letitia set about the activities she had been putting off. Then, on the following Saturday night, with her brother out and while she was watching television, the phone rang.

Putting her cup down on a small coffee-table beside her, she rose and went over to answer it, wondering who it could be ringing at this time of night. She said, 'Hello, Letitia here.'

For a moment there was only silence, then a voice

said, 'Yes, I know!'

And it was her turn to keep quiet. It was a voice that had said out there in front of his home while closing a car door, 'Until next time, Letitia,' but whose presence had been remarkable only by its absence. Of course she knew who it was, even with only that one sentence being spoken.

'Yes,' the voice said again, 'I know! I've rung to say that with Johnny putting in a crop quite soon, and although he has Mario to help him, it still might be a good idea for him to see the new way of picking and stringing, and the latest electric barns . . .'

'But we don't have electric barns. We only have the old-style wood-burning ones, as you . . .'

She was interrupted. 'Yes, I do know that, Letitia, and that it could be a couple of years before Johnny can get them. However, I have friends . . . relations of a sort, actually, who farm at Dimbulah. They planted in December, so they're picking now. I think it would do you both good to come along and watch.

'I also realise,' that cool, assured voice continued over the words she had begun to say, 'that Johnny has worked among tobacco, but not for quite some time . . . and farming is changing you know! So will you tell him about this, because I'm sure he'd want to come. And of course you're invited too. In fact I think you should both get some idea of the new technique.'

Oh yes, thought Letitia, she did know Johnny would be very happy to go. Anything that Dominic Catalano suggested, her young brother would gladly acquiesce to. But she wasn't her young brother; and some sort of instinct was telling her that danger lay about the person of this man as far as she herself was concerned. So now she said,

'Johnny isn't here.' She couldn't make herself call him Dominic, and she was just a bit apprehensive of calling him Mr Catalano as she remembered that handsome face whose expression had shown only charm and gaiety while he was dancing with her. He had called her Letitia after that. However, she also remembered with a slight shiver that different expression it had held while he looked her over in her pink shorts.

So now, using no name, she made herself say, 'Would you mind if perhaps this time we gave it a miss?'

'Yes, I'm afraid I would mind. I've made the arrangements because I was sure that was what Johnny would want to do. So just tell him to run that old jalopy of yours inside my gate. I'll be waiting there for you around nine. I'll see you then!' The line went dead.

Letitia had told Johnny; and of course they were going, one of them wanting to go or not. And also Dominic was right—it would be good experience for her brother. Her lips curled. This was the second time she had had to do what she didn't want to. And determinedly she had decided that this unexpected expedition was going to be the last time it was going to happen.

Today would be of benefit; but Johnny had Mario, and Peter had told them he was very good at his job. But for now, she finished dressing and allowed her glance to check the end product. Yes, she would do, she decided. She used foundation lavishly for protection against a sun they would probably be in, coloured her lips a little more deeply than usual for the same reason, her hair silken and shining as it swung free.

She might not be beautiful, or have that certain attraction that made heads turn for another look, but her figure was much more than just average. And the denim skirt and the white blouse with its raglan sleeves and high collar showed it off. She grinned suddenly, thinking that the apricot-tinted legs extending from beneath it weren't too bad either.

She turned from the mirror, and collecting her big shoulder-bag, left the room to make her way outside to wait. 'Hurry up, Johnny!' she called as she did so.

Gazing out upon the new day, a blue and golden day of which she saw nothing, she wondered why. Why was this man mixing into their lives; a man whose style of existence was so far removed from their own? She acknowledged that everything he had done had been helpful.

He had found Mario for them, the man they had been asked to that party to meet, and who now had his own small flat over near their farm buildings. But why?

Letitia turned as her brother came hurrying out, and, unable to prevent herself, smiled admiringly at him as he stood outlined against the vividness of a deep cerulean sky. He was dressed only in working jeans and a check shirt.

He saw her expression and grinned back. 'Didn't you look at yourself in the mirror this morning?' he asked. 'You could draw more wolf-whistles than ever I could!'

'As for that, I have Buckley's chance and my own,' was all she answered drily on that subject.

'I'm really looking forward to today. I expect to learn a lot,' Johnny said, and added, 'It will be great going in a Jaguar too, instead of our old wreck.'

'It's really not a wreck, Johnny,' protested Letitia, but she just received an unrepentant smile in return. 'And how,' she found herself forced to ask, 'do you know what kind of a car we're going in?'

'I told you, Dominic dropped young Vanni at the Club. Come on, we'd better get going.' Johnny picked up the carryall he had brought and led the way down the steps.

The car was waiting at the side of the road. And it *was* a Jaguar, long and grey! The gate was also standing open, and Johnny drove through. They walked back to where the tall man was standing beside an open car door. Johnny closed the gate behind them.

'Good morning.' An impartial smile passed between them both. Letitia's quiet reply was overshadowed by her brother's cheerful one. A hand indicated that he sit in the back; Letitia was handed into the front with more ceremony.

Dimbulah was only thirty miles away; a tobacco town like their own, if smaller, but Letitia had never been there. Johnny occasionally leaned over from his seat to answer a question or ask one. But Letitia mostly sat silent. Once she glanced sideways at their driver as he lounged against his seat, long tanned fingers resting lightly on the wheel. He wasn't dressed in jeans, she noticed, but in brown cords and one of those voile shirts he seemed to favour.

His head swung round as if he realised she was looking at him. And he smiled!

It was only a friendly smile, she told herself sharply, and turned swiftly away as she felt a tide of colour burn her cheeks. Good heavens, what would he think if he realised the way she had taken that smile? Dominic Catalano! Owning a farm and coffee estate ten times the size of theirs. Owning that big cluster of shops and offices occupying an entire corner block in the main street . . . and goodness knew what else besides. Letitia shook her head, made her breathing slow, and told herself not to be stupid—vowing that from now on she was going to act as she normally did, cool, calm, and collected.

They were passing a large farm on the northern outskirts of town, which Dominic pointed to, saying 'That's my uncle Joe's place.'

'You seem to have a lot of relatives, Dominic,' came from Johnny. 'And they all seem different.'

'Yes.' the silent girl in her corner felt the glance which passed over her as their driver half turned in his seat. He was continuing, 'My grandmother was an Australian, my grandfather an Italian. My mother married another Italian, hence me. My aunt Jean was a Norwegian Australian, hence Ben and Joe; and my uncle Joe married a Yugoslav, hence my three cousins—apart from the ones in Brisbane belonging to my grandmother's side. So you see, Johnny, we're quite a mixture.'

Johnny was interrupting, Letitia was smiling, and suddenly Dominic was laughing. 'Thank goodness we all speak English, though. It would be a United Nations day when we all get together, if we didn't,' he was finishing.

'The mixture doesn't seem to have done you or the two cousins I've met any harm. You're all attractive, handsome men . . .' Oh, lord, she thought, do I always have to say stupid things? Couldn't I just think them?

Had Dominic taken notice of what she had said? If so, it didn't seem he was going to comment on it. All she could see of him was that sculptured profile as he gazed intently at the road unwinding before him. And if Johnny had heard, his mind was evidently thinking of other things. He was chatting away to Dominic.

Then Dominic was saying, 'Here we are! We don't need to go through into the town,' as he swung into a side road.

It couldn't be! thought Letitia with a startled glance at her wristwatch. It wasn't half an hour since they had started. Then she remembered that Dimbulah was only thirty miles from Mareeba. Of course, Dominic would drive those thirty miles, in this car, in under half an hour.

Tobacco was now growing on both sides of their swiftly moving vehicle, running away into the distance. This was a big farm, and the house when they passed it was modern, low-set, painted pristine white. One like many you saw on the farms around—the wealthy farms, but very unlike Dominic's villa.

Pulling up before a multitude of buildings, the towering tobacco barns overshadowing them all, Dominic said, 'We thought we wouldn't go over to the house for morning tea. That would probably turn the day into a social event, not the working day we want for Johnny . . .' He broke off, turning to greet the two men advancing towards them. 'Hi, Riccardo, Giulio,' he said.

'Come on, Dominic! You "Riccardo" me just once again and you'll find yourself in the river . . . heaved there by me! Hello there,' the younger one was continuing, but speaking now to his two younger visitors. 'I'm Rick, or Ricky, take your pick, and this is my father, Giulio Panizzi. I think Dad has some tea and coffee for you, but I'm afraid I'll have to give it a miss—we're too busy! Coming, Johnny?' He grinned across at the boy. Evidently everything *had* been arranged.

Yes, of course Johnny was coming! Tea held no attraction for him at this moment. Letitia watched them go out of the enormous, high working space between buildings; her Johnny and Rick, as she supposed she had better call him, who was clad in stained khaki shorts and a khaki shirt which could have come from the ragbag. But another handsome connection of Dominic's, it seemed.

And it was with Dominic's fingers under her elbow, piloting her, that she walked towards a bench. 'Tea or coffee?' the older man was asking, and she replied,

'Tea, please,' then added smilingly as he made to take hold of a dainty china cup and saucer, 'One of those mugs will do. I grew up on a tobacco farm, you know, and drank tea in between picking and stringing. Mugs, and the bigger they were the better, were what we used.'

'Yes, I suppose you did. And owning a tobacco farm, there's only one thing that matters, isn't there? Being among it and working it! But you're a visitor today, so I'd better do as my wife tells me.' He filled a small teacup and passed it across, accompanied by flaky Italian pastries, then turned away as a call came from outside.

'Yes, I expect you're right,' was all she answered.

'Little liar,' came from above her head, and she turned startled eyes on her companion.

'You don't like tobacco, Letitia. It's in your tone when you speak of it.'

'That's not true, Dominic,' she protested. 'It's not that I don't like it—and who would dare not to in this locality where tobacco is king?—it's just that I don't like the smell of it getting into my hair; which it does do when we're working among it. And I bet I'm the only one who doesn't like it for such a silly reason. These people obviously love it.' She made a throwaway gesture to the enormous space about them, the innumerable green paddocks glinting in the sunshine. 'And Johnny certainly does . . .' She broke off as their host returned.

Dominic said, 'You've got a lot of tobacco in, Giulio. You haven't thought of diversifying yet?'

'No, I haven't! We've discussed that before! Let others do that if they want to,' grinned Giulio, white teeth showing in the dark face as he added, 'The less tobacco they put in, the better it is for us. When you're talking about a quarter of a million dollars crop, or even more, every year, you don't fool around with it.'

Dominic shrugged, but didn't have to reply, because abruptly the entire area around them was a hive of activity. Lorries had driven up, stretchers full of tobacco leaf were being hauled in. And, standing back, Letitia saw stringing machines in action for the first time.

Watching, she said to her companion, forgetting for the moment who he was, 'I used to very good at stringing,' and the remembered actions came back as she saw pole after pole being strung—a swift, special turn of string, a hand of tobacco hanging down one side of the thin wooden stick, another twist of string, and a second hand of leaf hung on the other side. But of course the machine was much faster.

'Johnny will want one of these,' she said fatalistically, and Dominic laughed.

'Yes, I expect he will, but tell him to wait a while, because I've heard there's a new process for curing tobacco in the pipeline; we'll just have to wait and see how it works. As they say, progress is an ongoing event.'

The sticks of tobacco were being shouldered over to a big barn for curing, and Letitia saw her brother turn from the stringing machine and walk over to examine that.

'And,' she said emphatically, 'if he thinks he's going to get an electric barn before he discovers how good he is at growing tobacco, he has another think coming. Thank goodness I'm his guardian for the next seven months!'

More than a soft amused laugh came from Dominic this time, and still laughing, he took hold of her arm and said, 'Come along out of this madhouse.'

He flipped a lock of fair, shining hair with a tanned finger, adding, 'We can't have this smelling of tobacco, now can we?'

She went with him because she had no choice, and leaving the busy scene behind them, they strolled through paddock after paddock of living green. Arriving at the river, Dominic said, 'It's the same river that we have, but I always think it's bigger and deeper.'

Always, afterwards, when she remembered that day, Letitia recalled it as a time filled with Dominic's presence. They had walked by the river. They had watched the irrigation jets send their sparkling rainbows of water high in the air over crops not yet ready for harvesting. They had sat down to an enormous lunch, among what seemed an enormous amount of people too. They had even gone into Dimbulah with the Jaguar full of youngsters.

Then the every-minute-filled, dreamlike day was ended, and they were on their way home, accompanied by a violent sunset which stained the horizon with crimson and scarlet. Letitia sat quietly in the swiftly moving car and watched as the vivid colours gradually faded to deep orange, then to the palest lavender. Then, suddenly, they had gone, and as the big vehicle ate up the miles, they were driving into evening.

'Dominic,' Johnny spoke as they neared home, 'I'll get my jalopy out of your driveway if you'll wait a moment. Then I'll take Letitia home before I go to Atherton to collect Mario. He had to go there for the weekend, so I told him I'd collect him.' He was out of the car, talking as he went, unwilling to keep their driver waiting.

'Calm down, Johnny, will you? But certainly get your car, and if you're going all that way, don't go on as you are now.' Dominic's voice was more curt than Letitia had ever heard it speak. 'Take it a bit more slowly. There's no reason to be in a hurry; nor is there any need to take your sister home. I'll run her there, as she's already in the car.'

'OK, thanks very much.' Her brother had turned his wide, happy smile on their driver, before trotting off to open the gate. He leaned out of his window as he drove past and said, 'See you, Sis.'

Dominic drove slowly as if he had something on his mind. Then in just a few minutes the Jaguar was pulling into their own driveway. It came to a stop at the side of the house and, descending, Letitia saw that the first faint twinkling of stars were beginning to show in a pale blue sky. But as her companion came to stand beside her, twilight was abruptly gone, allowing the darkness of night to take over.

Dominic held out a hand for the key she had just finished rummaging for in her bag, and automatically she handed it to him, although this was the only time in her life she had been called on to do such a thing. He inserted the key effortlessly and swung the door open. He didn't stand aside to allow her to enter, however; he went first and switched on the light.

Moving before him as he stood back, Letitia heard the front door close and Dominic moving closely behind her. It was she who switched on the big fluorescent one above the kitchen half of the long room, not bothering to turn on the lounge light. She turned to him, reaching out a hand to take her keys, and started to say her thank-yous for the lift. But laying them down on a small coffee table, Dominic said, 'May I?'

And again, automatically, she nodded without knowing what he wanted. He left her, and moving through the hall, switched on every light in every room as he went.

She was actually sporting a grin when he returned, and forgetting he was who he was, said prosaically, 'You really didn't think there'd be any burglars in here, did you, Dominic?'

'No, I don't expect so. However . . . you are a young girl, coming home to an empty house situated in a rather empty neighbourhood. I really don't think that should be the case, Letitia.'

'Don't be silly!' and as she spoke her hand flew to her mouth as if to stop the words escaping, and over it she found herself looking directly into his wide-open gaze.

CHAPTER FOUR

BUT thankfully she saw that those green eyes were smiling; no enigmatic look coloured their expression this time. Dominic said, however, before she could continue, 'I'm not being silly. I still think what I said was right.'

'But look—I've lived here all my life. We know most of the people around here. There's never been any . . . any unpleasantness at all. Such a thing has never even crossed my mind.'

'Still, before, you had . . .' Dominic paused for a moment before continuing, 'your grandfather was here until just recently. Now it's different.'

'No, it is not!' Impatience coloured the words. 'Johnny is here, don't forget.'

'I'm not forgetting, and I'll make it my business to see that either he or Mario is here at night.'

Astonished, almost amazed, Letitia looked up at him, then spoke, and didn't realise the astringency in her voice. 'This is being silly! As I said, I've never even thought of anyone breaking into this place.' She spared a glance for the darkness showing through the big glass doors opening on to the veranda, before adding tartly, 'And I'm not going to start thinking about it now.'

Her tone changing quickly, she spoke again. 'Can I get you a drink, Dominic? I know,' she was smiling pleasantly at him now, 'that you do drink beer, which is all the alcohol we have.'

For the fraction of a second the man across from her hesitated—she saw it. Then he answered, a smile in both voice and eyes, 'I wouldn't like a drink, thank you, but I wouldn't mind a cup of tea.' Her expression must have shown her astonishment, because he added, 'I know it's getting on for dinnertime, but I couldn't face up to that just yet—after that whopping lunch they force-fed us up at the farm today. However, I really would like a cup of tea.'

'Fair enough,' she answered, then turned from where she had moved towards the kitchen part of the room, adding with an eyebrow raised, 'Truly tea? I know you . . . Italians mostly drink coffee.'

'Yes, we Italians do mostly drink coffee, but I'm different. I drink tea! I was brought up by my grandmother, you see; my mother I hardly remember. And my grandmother was one of the old-time Australians; tea was the staff of life to her.'

'Oh!' was all Letitia could find to answer this unexpected and, to her, astonishing news. Then before she could stop herself, she blurted out, 'You even speak a little bit differently too. Is that because of her?' Then a hand flew to her mouth, and she decided yet again that she could never keep her wretched mouth closed.

But Dominic was laughing. She heard it, and thought, This is the first time I've heard him laughing out loud with amusement. He was also saying, 'Yes, I expect it is. My mother used to speak like that too, they tell me.'

Switching on the kettle, she wondered what answer she would get if she asked him if that was where he got the colour of his eyes. And it was while thinking of that that she swung suddenly round and met his gaze. For the space of a heartbeat there was that straight line of tension between them again, the same one which had occurred before, on the veranda of his own home. There, Dominic had remained motionless for a brief moment before casually turning to walk away. Now, he had deliberately moved to sit lounging sideways at the table, long legs outstretched.

Letitia moved over to a dresser set against the wall. She took down two large breakfast cups and saucers, collected teaspoons from a drawer, and with a wry grin moved over to the table. *She* wasn't going to walk down to the other end of the room to get out fragile bone china for a kitchen cup of tea. He would have to like or lump ordinary breakfast cups.

Giving those outstretched legs a wide berth, she set the crockery down, beginning to say, 'Would you like something to eat . . .?' but was interrupted by an up-lifted negative hand before she could finish the sentence. She went back to stand by the nearly boiling kettle.

She said into a small unnerving silence, 'It was a wonderful day for Johnny today, and he did learn a lot of things, didn't he, Dominic?'

'It certainly was, and yes, he did,' answered the man sitting with his eyelids hooding most of his eyes.

'And tobacco is definitely going to be his crop. I caught him looking at a leaf he held in his hand today . . . he was stroking it as if he was caressing it.' Astringency coloured her voice now as she continued, 'Can you imagine such a thing?'

Across from her, lids suddenly lifted from emerald green eyes, and a pirate's glance was being directed at her. Laughing, wickedly brilliant, those eyes held her gaze—then unexpectedly, as if a recollection had surfaced, they were as suddenly hooded. And when they opened wide again, they held only a smiling pleasantness.

'Oh, yes, I can imagine such a thing. Attraction makes strange bedfellows; hasn't the world reason to know that? But about Johnny—you've no need to worry about him,' he was answering her question. 'It's good for a boy to know what he wants to do. Look at all the years I have, and I'm just beginning to find out what I really want.'

Letitia couldn't understand that strange nuance colouring his voice. 'You can't have lived here in Mareeba very much, Dominic,' she interposed. 'I don't remember you at all.' She didn't say, and I would have, but she thought it.

'No, I went away to school when I was eleven—my grandmother's rules. Then, after school I went on to agricultural college for another three years. Now, while Giovanni is the tobacco expert, coffee is my baby.'

Letitia was doing mental arithmetic in her mind while warming the pot and making the tea, wondering exactly how old he was.

As if reading her thoughts, he said, 'I'll be thirty at the end of the year. Time to stop my wandering and settle down, or at least, that's what my family are always saying. The trouble is . . .' He stopped sharply as if he was unwilling to continue on with that subject, then he did continue.

'I *have* been wandering . . . all over the world! England first, then Europe, then Brazil. Because I thought even then that coffee would be the crop to suit this particular climate. Look,' he interrupted himself, 'how did we get on to this subject? It's of no interest to anyone else!'

'Oh, please,' she pleaded, wanting desperately for him to continue, and added, 'Here's your tea, but please go on. I've seen so little of the world out there. Did you like England?'

'Yes, I liked England very much, and believe me, I saw a lot of it. And Europe . . . including of course, Italy! I hadn't realised, although I should have, by the number of letters my grandmother wrote, how many of my grandfather's relations she kept in touch with. And I think I met them all. Oh, yes, I certainly saw Italy!'

'And I think,' here those eyes of his laughed across at her, 'it was there that, for my own protection, I learnt to keep my eyes as closed as I could manage. At home they were taken for granted, coming from my Australian grandmother's side of the family. She had them, so does my aunt Jean. But in Italy . . .!'

'Oh, so that's why your eyelids fall at certain times . . .' Letitia broke off again, furious with herself.

'I expect you could say that. Constantly practising a thing does tend to make it become a habit.'

Letitia shook her head, saying only, 'I can't understand this attitude about your eyes, Dominic. They're . . .' This time she thanked whatever fates there were that she had managed to stop her unruly tongue, before uttering what she had been thinking.

'Thank you very much, Letitia, for your forbearance.' Dominic was laughing out loud now, all reminiscence gone with the wind. He made to rise. He said, 'I'd better be going, I've stayed much longer than I should have.'

As she rose quickly also as he spoke, thinking that of course it might have been boring for him—this, to her, so fascinating interlude—her outflung arm caught the teapot, sending it sliding across the slippery laminated table-top. She had no chance of catching it. It fell, leaving in its wake a stain of dark khaki across Dominic's fawn cords; trousers that were still immaculate even after an entire day of traipsing about a farm and its crops.

Aghast, she snatched up a tea-towel from off the rack and made to pat the spreading marks. It wasn't a case of the fluid being hot; the tea had long cooled. It was the dreadful brown stain on pristine material that caused her look of anguish.

'Stop it, Letitia!' Two hands were hard upon her shoulders, holding her away. 'It doesn't matter! I said, leave it!' His words echoed harshly, the voice strange.

Gripped by those hands—they stood only inches apart, gazing directly at each other—Letitia saw the eyes wide open now, pupils concentrated into diamond pinpoints. An entirely new sensation, a jolting shock, reached out to her, and she swayed—not away, but towards him.

'No!' said Dominic in that still strange voice, and his hands dropped from her shoulders, pushing her away.

She did move, but the hesitant pace was again towards him.

His hands came once more to clasp on her shoulders, and across so tiny a space that unknown jolting shock ran zigzagging. Then his fingers were slipping down, slowly, caressingly, along bare, smooth arms. And as they passed it seemed to Letitia that every nerve-end she possessed stood exposed. She shivered. Clasped finally at the wrist, his hands brought her to him.

Only lightly touching, she stood against the tall masculine figure, length to his length, but the tautness, the tension from it flowed over her. Then his hands left her wrists, one reaching around, one to rest lying against her throat, and as she waited, silent in a silent room, his head came down.

The lips that came to rest upon her own were not hard, not violent or demanding. They were warm and moved caressingly against them. With a deep, surrendering sigh, Letitia stretched up on rubber-soled walking shoes, sliding her arms to clasp them tightly behind his neck. And as if that small surrender had touched off a desire until now kept in check, his arm went low, spreadeagling hard against her back, bringing her into him. She didn't know she had gasped; she didn't hear the small sound. She was only aware of a body that was part of her body, that hollows and curves were merging and fusing into one whole.

She wasn't thinking now; the space around her was vanishing, as those slow, heartbreaking kisses began to turn her very bones to wanting, needing . . . Her hands about Dominic's neck went tighter, her twisting form moving even more close—until the only thing between their stretched bodies was the muffled thud of Dominic's heartbeats echoing between them.

Letitia felt, rather than knew, when those lips seemingly drawing the soul from her body had moved. They were travelling along her jawline over an exposed throat, to stop at the bare, cool skin which the cleavage of a loose blouse had left uncovered.

Her body collapsed against him as his lips caressed the soft smoothness. Head thrown back over his arm, silver-gilt hair cascading down on it, she was unaware of anything but the unwinding coils of desire and passion reaching through her entire body. Then those expert, experienced lips moved, but so slowly, stopping on their way to cover a throbbing pulse that jumped and jumped.

On her mouth again, the demand was growing as his lips moved gently and sensuously back and forth across her own, and she knew she murmured somewhere deep inside her, 'Dominic . . . Dominic . . .'

She was abruptly swept up, and her captor was striding swiftly towards the dimly lit lounge. There she was set on the sofa. She lay flat, her glance hazed with that soaring passion which was still a memory within it.

The man sat beside her, hands stretched rigid on either side, making a prisoner of her. His gaze was carrying its own share of the desire which had engulfed them, but his expression was also showing a certain wryness.

'I really am out of bounds,' he said. 'I came in here to see that everything was safe for you—and look how I behave!'

Letitia shook her head. His name was all she could answer. And it was *her* voice that was strange now. She reached up a hand to stroke down the dark cheek with the back of her fingers, marvelling that she was actually able to do such a thing. She said again only, 'Dominic . . .' and her body arched up to him.

Slowly, as if unwillingly, he bent over her, the heavy solid length of him, and as their lips met and merged, desire flaring, she knew that this time there would be no turning back. Because now that heavy, long body was not looming above; it was along her side, its whole hard length fusing into the curves and hollows melting in softness to receive it. The hand that was not cradling her to him worked its own magic as it trailed up and down, across and over her unresistant form. It came to rest on a bare, naked thigh . . . and halted abruptly. She felt it spread flat, the long fingers warm against it, and she turned her body more to him.

Then suddenly, unexpectedly, without understanding the reason for it, she felt the atmosphere around their two clasped forms change, and abruptly Dominic had swung off the couch to stand sharply upright. He walked the few steps to the closed doors to stand gazing through the heavy glass into the night.

Abandoned, lying there, she hadn't understood that forcefully uttered expletive which had accompanied Dominic's withdrawal—it had been sharply spoken in Italian. She swung off the couch and with shaking legs leaned against the wooden back of it. She said huskily, 'I apologise, Dominic . . . I'm sorry, it was my fault.' And, fatalistically, she knew that it had been. 'Now will you please go! That's all I want you to do now!'

For a second longer he remained beside the glass panes, then drawing a deep breath, his chest rising sharply with his seeming need for extra air, he walked across to face her.

'Don't be foolish, Letitia—of course it wasn't your fault. The fault is that I shouldn't be here. I should have known better. There was no excuse for it. Now——' he reached out a hand to her, but she drew back, cringing away from it.

She knew she couldn't bear to have him touch her. She said again, 'I want you to go. Please go now!' She moved further away, the sofa between them a barrier.

The expression on the face of the man standing before her changed. That sculptured mouth which had been curved with gentleness thinned, a cruel, ruthless line coming to take its place, those brilliant emerald eyes narrowing to the merest slits, as the tone of his voice returned to the clipped timbre of its normal tone. 'I have already told you, Letitia, not to be foolish. Look, I also want to tell you, you don't realise the consequences . . .' Again long fingers reached out to clasp one of her hands resting on the sofa back for support. And again she drew back sharply, her arm snaking away behind her back.

She forced her glance away from him, making it look blankly over his shoulder. She said jerkily, 'I want you to go. I only want you to go, please.'

For a silent moment after that husky plea reached out to him, Dominic gazed directly into her face, then his shoulders went up in a shrug. He replied briskly, 'All right, I'll go now, but I have things to say to you tomorrow. I'll see you then.' He waited a moment and, receiving no answer, turned and walked down the hallway.

Letitia heard the front door open, then slam shut with a decisively loud click. She still remained motionless until the soft purr of the Jaguar came to her out of the still night. Then, with a ragged breath, making her body stand upright by itself, she picked up her keys and bag, and went towards the haven of her bedroom.

She sank on to the bed, the thought of Johnny's arrival home surfacing. She wanted to talk to nobody about the previous hour. She walked swiftly through the house, flipping out lights that other fingers had turned on, and in the bathroom stood under a cascade of warm, streaming water, her face raised to it as if to wash away the memory of any touch that might have lingered there.

Out of the shower, she wrapped herself in a towel
and flipped out the light, doing the same in her
bedroom. Then, patting herself dry in a room illuminated only with outside starshine, she pulled on a short
cotton nightdress and climbed into bed. There she
curled up, pulling the sheet and then the thin blanket
folded at the foot of the bed about her tensely knotted
body.

She didn't want to think of Dominic. She wished she
could wipe the last hour completely away and make her
mind a blank. She shut her eyes, and immediately that
dark, handsome face was there looking at her. Restlessly she turned—she knew she would have to think
about it, come to some sensible reaction or reason, if she
was to face tomorrow.

How in the name of heaven had it all started, that
cataclysmic event coming right out of the blue? It had
been such a wonderful day, and he had been such a big
part of it. A pleasant and smiling host on the drive to
Dimbulah; a pleasant acquaintance too, the times he
had spoken and smiled to her at the farm. And . . . and
even tonight; that had been fun, and the talk about
other countries so fascinating. And also that laughing
explanation of how the Italians thought of his eyes—
those marvellous eyes she would never see light up for
her again . . . so what had started it? When she had
knocked the teapot over him, she supposed.

He would have gone . . . he would have left the
house. Absolutely Letitia knew that—if she hadn't
moved towards him. What in the name of heaven must
he think of her? She turned her face into the pillow. To
throw herself at him as she had done!

This was today's world, she realised that. But
Dominic Catalano didn't strike her as a man moving in
free and easy circles. Oh, he had wanted to make love
to her; she didn't doubt it. Inexperienced in such
matters as she was, that was one fact she knew

absolutely. Her eyes closed without her telling them to do so as she remembered . . . She shook her head sharply to stop this kind of thinking. Oh yes, Dominic had wanted her. What man wouldn't, given the way she had responded?

But even through those passionate caresses which had been sending them both into only one dimension, that of complete desire, a thought must have struck him. Being who he was, and, as he had told her tonight, almost thirty, of course he would have commitments. He would undoubtedly have women friends—or even a mistress, she told herself vindictively. Remembering the way he had made love, remembering the warm, slow, heartbreaking kisses, the experienced caresses that had sent her every nerve clamouring to meet his wishes, she decided, again vindictively, that he probably had *two* mistresses.

Then, if she could be said to smile on this unhappy night, a tiny one surfaced at the age-old designation she had used for naming what was, in this new age, called merely a girlfriend or lover.

Still—she cringed inside herself again. What must Dominic be thinking of her? He had known her a bare three weeks, and how many times had they actually met? Three, without counting today, and she had let him . . .

Oh, lord! And he was an Italian—well, mostly Italian. And they had definite ideas on morality . . . or they had about their own women's morality. What was it he had said? The fact is, I shouldn't be here. I should have known better!

Letitia straightened out from the cramped position she had rolled herself into. She knew she was in love with him. She knew now that she would never want any other man to hold, to kiss, to touch her, as Dominic Catalano had done. But she had a life to live, and she would manage, thank you very much!

The money her grandfather had saved would enable her to leave Mareeba as soon as Johnny was settled. And of course she would! There was a whole world out there, and she would find herself a niche in it.

Finding she had at last managed to contrive some semblance of calm, she decided it was no use thinking of that humiliating scene just past in which she had thrown herself at a man who didn't want her. So she lay still, endeavouring to woo sleep.

She heard the car arrive home; she heard Johnny and Mario laughing, then call goodnight to one another. She heard her brother come inside and ask, 'Are you asleep, Sis?' and, receiving no answer, poke his head around her half-open door, then, apparently satisfied that she was there and safe, make off to his own room. He didn't shower, and he must have undressed in minutes flat, because the light went out, the house returning to darkness and silence.

Letitia lay, unable to sleep, watching the dark hours slide by, and thinking there was one thing she knew. If, and it was probably only an if, Dominic did come here the next day, he wouldn't find her here.

CHAPTER FIVE

THERE was a cool breeze blowing off the sea. Not enough, however, to make the girl sitting on the bench reach for the cardigan she carried. After all, it was only the middle of April, and the mild winter of this far northern land didn't really begin until another month.

She leaned against the slatted railings at her back, happy to be just here with all thought held at bay, with the shimmering waves of a blue scintillating ocean dancing and sparkling before her. It was a tourist brochure scene she was looking at. A small mountain thickly clothed in green rose to one side, and in front, stretching into the far distance was a sheet of vivid gleaming cerulean. Palm trees shivered and rattled their branches in the offshore breeze as they stood starkly outlined against the jumble of city buildings behind them.

Letitia knew she would have to get up and go back to reality soon. It was getting late and she had to shop; the excuse she had given to Johnny for her unexpectedly early departure down the range to Cairns.

She did know she would have to go back. Dinner had to be preared; Johnny was working hard and needed good meals. But she didn't want to meet Dominic again—definitely not, not after last night. But if he actually had gone to the farm this morning as he had stated he would, he wouldn't come again after finding her gone. That was for certain.

Giving a last appreciative glance at the sunlit, dancing water, she knew that just watching the small lazy blue wavelets had worked its own kind of soothing magic.

But now she really would have to go. She would go and buy the dress which had been the excuse for this trip. There was that special farmers' day coming along, which Johnny had told her she would have no reason now for not attending, so she would look for as lovely a dress as she could find. And . . . she thought it would be most unlikely that Dominic would be going to such an affair.

So, with a last look about her, she strolled slowly to where she had left the car, and knew that from now on she had better pay more attention to the outside world, not to the one within her. Traffic was heavy and she had to find a parking slot—which might not be the easiest thing to do. And then, quite unexpectedly, one was in front of her. As she slid triumphantly between the cars on either side, she didn't realise that for a brief moment the dark cloud that had seemed to engulf her since last night slid away from her expression at this tiny slice of good fortune.

Browsing through a big department store, she decided there were lovely dresses on display, but none that took her fancy. So she rode the escalator and began to saunter along to a boutique she knew of . . . when there it was! She stopped, her gaze enchanted as it fell upon the one dress outspread in a window display. She glanced up and, spying the name on the façade, almost turned away . . . and then looked at the dress again.

After all, she had all that money, and she had really only splurged on so few things. Another glance at the tangerine creation decided her. She went into the shop, and the salesgirl came smiling towards her. Letitia said, 'I'd like to see if that dress in the window is my size.'

'Certainly.' The girl was pleasant; however she looked Letitia over—a girl casually dressed in flared skirt and a loose white overblouse. 'It is a beautiful dress,' she said, then smiled to take away any sting as she added, 'but it's very expensive.'

As Letitia made no reply, she turned away to tenderly

lift the creation from out of the window. Before addressing her customer again, she turned over a small tag dangling from it. Casually she named the price, then said, 'It is your size. Do you want to try it on?'

Exhaling carefully, thinking that at least she had managed not to literally turn and run when the amount was mentioned, Letitia grinned, saying, 'Yes, please.'

In the changing room, the dress spread before her, she knew if it fitted she was going to buy it, no matter what. The material shone dully as if it had gold threads interwoven in its tangerine stiffness, yet it could be worn in the daytime, or at night.

Made with a shirtwaist top that was clasped with jade buttons; three-quarter-length sleeves, having a button of the same colour fastening stiffened cuffs, it also had a stiffened collar standing high at the back.

Eased over her head, the full gathered skirt swung about her, while a two-inch-wide belt pulled tight showed the slimness of her waist. She said to the woman helping her, 'You wouldn't expect the belt and button colour to match the tangerine, would you?'

'Oh, but look at the maker's label. That's the reason it's the price it is . . . because of the design.' The girl stood back, watching Letitia twist and turn before the mirror. With that expression on the face of her client, she knew there was no need to try and sell it.

But suddenly, abruptly, that happy smile was wiped completely from the face looking at the reflection before her. The salesgirl had lightly touched where the first button was fastened. 'The cleavage is cut a little low,' she remarked, 'but that's the fashion today. And really,' she smiled gaily, 'it's so discreetly cut that it's a marvellous plus.'

But blindingly, out of the blue, Letitia remembered a dark head bending low over her; lips that had rested exactly there where the low cleavage began.

She bent sharply down, as if to search in her

handbag, then upright again, blonde hair hanging every which way around a face having an excuse for pink cheeks, and began to take off the dress.

'You know, actually I wouldn't have said offhand that this is your colour,' she was being told, 'but . . .' and this time the smile on the other girl's face was open and friendly, 'if you can afford it, it *is* your dress! You look fabulous . . . and will look even more so when you're made up and dressed to go out. You'll wow them!'

'No, I don't think I'll do that. But yes, I'm very pleased, and I'm happy with how it suits me.' Letitia finished removing it and handing it over while speaking.

Dressed, she combed her hair, then went to stand by a counter where her invoice was being made out. She wrote the cheque, and watched the dress being packed away in tissue paper in one of the silver and cream boxes that was a trademark of this particular boutique. As she handed it over to her, the girl behind the counter said, 'What shoes are you going to wear?'

Puzzled for a moment, her mind thinking of something she was trying not to think about, it was only absently that Letitia answered. 'I have a practically new pair of high-heeled white sandals. I expect I'll wear them . . .' and she broke off as the salesgirl shook her head emphatically.

'Oh, no, you can't wear them!' she was saying in a scandalised tone. 'This is an exclusive dress, you understand. You must wear shoes that match—either the colour of the buttons or a tangerine or orange shade . . .' She came to an abrupt halt, saying, 'Sorry, it's just that you'd spoil the whole look of it if you wear . . .'

Again she broke off and looked apologetically at Letitia, who was suddenly laughing, thoughts of Dominic scattered—for the moment! All the money she had ever spent on shoes was for the special boots she needed when she worked her mangoes. They were a necessity. For the rest, they had come off a chain store rack.

She began to laugh again. She said, 'Would white sandals really not do?' Receiving only a deprecatory shrug, she sighed, 'OK, I'll think about it.'

Outside, she was still smiling. She glanced down at the ornate box swinging at her side, and muttered, 'Why not?'

Up the block and around the corner, she wended her way along the crowded footpath and entered the wide, large opening of a shoe shop. She gazed about her at what seemed millions of them, then walked purposefully to the back of the shop. Yes, there they were, on stands along the wall, each pair in splended isolation. And with the mild winter months in the offing, they were mostly closed shoes—in all sorts of colours.

Once again outside, still smiling, Letitia gazed down at the other parcel swinging from a finger. They *did* match, almost exactly, and again she was happy with her purchase—high-heeled, but not too high; brushed pale green suede, with a simple cross-over in front to draw attention to their expensive simplicity.

Her wrist came up. Twenty to three—no time for eating. It was more than a couple of hours' drive home at the pace she drove. But first, what could she splurge on for Johnny? It wouldn't be clothes Johnny would want, not for a year or so, anyway. But she knew precisely what he *would* want.

So again she walked around another corner, searching for a shop. However, this one she was familiar with. And a third time she was out on the street carrying a large cardboard box. But this container couldn't be swung at her side on a piece of string. She carried it carefully in her arms.

Almost arriving at her car, she felt a hand catch at her arm. 'Letitia,' said a voice, and she turned quickly.

'You know,' quoted the smiling, good-lookng young man facing her, 'I really didn't know if it was you. I've only seen you at your farmers' "do"s. But . . .' a finger flicked at the fair shining hair, 'no one could miss that, even in this rushing crowd around us.' An outflung arm gestured to the busy, closely moving populace.

Richard was a colleague of Peter's and Letitia had met him quite a few times, so she smiled back at the laughing, attractive face. He had ade more than one pass at her, but finding she was not interested in his practised dalliance, that she didn't go to dances or parties a lot, he had decided that a friendly smile was all that was necessary on meeting.

'Hey, let me help you,' he said now, taking the large cardboard box from her arms. 'Is your car far away?'

'No, it's only three or four further down. But don't you dare drop that! It's a chocolate gâteau for Johnny.'

'Lucky Johnny! Still, they might serve such concoctions at that farmers' weekend in two weeks' time.'

Letitia pulled to a sudden stop, the face turned towards him carrying a frown between her brows. 'It isn't in just two weeks' time, surely?' she asked, and receiving a nod, thought, Well, two weeks is plenty of time for me to learn to school my expression . . . and my actions. She said casually, 'I wonder where we'll be going, and to what sort of farm?' She began walking again.

Fumbling the keys from her big bag, she told her escort, 'Put that parcel carefully on the back seat, please, Richard,' and when he had done so and began to move away from the door, she threw the other two boxes after it. However, his hand reached out and ran a finger over the name—blazoned outstandingly on one of the packages.

'Buying up, I see. Dare we hope that you might come along to the dinner dance afterwards? I was speaking . . .' here Richard paused for a moment and then continued carefully, 'to Peter, and he told me you might be going out a bit more. So how about saving me a dance?'

Letitia glanced up into his face and decided there was no time like the present to begin schooling her expression and actions, so she laughed and told him, 'Maybe . . . if I'm there. And maybe, if I have enough energy left, after traipsing around a farm all afternoon.'

'Oh, you'll have plenty of energy left. I'll see we pick an easy farm—something like a strawberry one. How about that?'

Letitia grinned back at him. 'Oh, that'll be fine, as long as you supply the cream,' she answered, laughing. 'But, for now, I've got to be off.' She slammed shut the door, waved a hand, and turned the key.

She hadn't seen a man making to get out of a long grey vehicle parked half a dozen cars or so away when he saw her coming, or his return to his seat when she was accosted by Richard. She didn't see, either, the expression on his face change, going from pleasantness to ruthlessness, as the lips thinned completely, and the eyelids fell over glinting emerald eyes. They remained half shut as he watched the laughing, intimate encounter being played so openly only a few yards distance.

Nor did she see the car pull out when she did, keeping some few vehicles between them as it followed. It fell back even further when they came to the mountain road which twisted and turned up to the tablelands beyond.

Letitia took it carefully. She had no intention of going over the side—to fall down for ever at some of the places. She put her foot down a little more heavily, though, on arriving at the top of the range, and beginning to head for home.

The two men were still at work among the crop when she pulled into the garage. Mario, the nearest, came over. 'We're finishing now,' he told her. 'Johnny says we just want to get this paddock done before we knock off. We'll only be half an hour or so, OK?'

'Yes, fine, Mario,' she answered his swiftly retreating back, and carried her parcels inside. She thought once again how lucky they were in getting Mario, and knew without having to think who they had to thank for that. Oh, well—she gave a wry grin—wasn't there some saying she could remember a bit of, about its being an ill wind that blew nobody any good?

And later she told her brother as he began to stack dishes, 'Leave them, Johnny. You've been working all day. Go and watch television. I'll clear away when I've finished my tea.'

Johnny rose. He looked down at her as she sat there, teacup held in both hands, and said, 'It's not that I've been working all day. The thing is that I'm just too full for anything except to sit down. Why didn't you have some?' he added, looking happily at what was left of the gateau. 'It was——' he paused for a moment, apparently searching for a word, 'absolutely scrumptious!' He blew a kiss from his fingertips to the air about them.

Letitia glanced at the large half of the cream and chocolate concoction which was left, and shuddered. Not that normally she didn't like such things—she did! But tonight, and also today, she had found that even the thought of food caused her throat to tighten completely. It was just nerves, she knew that, and she would get over it.

A shadow passed outside on the lighted veranda, and a hand was raised to knock on the glass door. She gazed with outraged anger at Dominic as he walked in. Handing over a large carton to Johnny who had risen to greet him, he nodded and said,

'Giovanni sent these over for Mario, and he also thought, Letitia,' he added to the silent girl at the table, 'that you might be able to use some as well. We know,' he gestured with a throwaway action, 'you have paw-paws and oranges and other such trees. But mostly you don't bother to grow salad vegetables as we do. So Giovanni picked enough for both of you.'

Letitia still continued to look silently at him, the outrage in her eyes a living thing. But he spoke to Johnny in that pleasant voice he could assume. 'Don't disturb yourself from the television. I'll just speak to Letitia for a minute, then I must be off.' He looked at her and then at the teapot, and, furiously angry, she saw that wicked pirate's expression come to glint from those vivid wide-open eyes. She would have liked to pick up the pot and throw the tea all over him—over those beautiful perfect clothes that he always wore.

Dominic must have seen the thought in her gaze. A hand went up, palm flatly exposed in the universal gesture of peace. 'Oh, no, Letitia,' he said softly 'these are good clothes. I wouldn't dare take them home ruined.'

With a quick glance that saw her brother engrossed in the television, she demanded through clenched teeth, 'What are you doing here? You're not wanted!'

That wicked, glinting smile departed, and only a pleasant acquaintance looked back at her. It said, 'I'll only detain you for a minute. And,' as she moved restlessly, 'I'm not going to apologise for what happened last night. I do want to ask you, though, would you just let things be for a while and be friends? Do you think you could manage that?

'Actually, however . . .' he continued as he received

no reply, with that glinting look once more a part of his expression. Letitia wondered suddenly, almost with fright, what he was thinking of to bring that gaze back again. 'Actually . . .' he was repeating, 'you might have to be friends with me, because I've been co-opted to take a party to that farmers' weekend that's coming off soon. It's been suggested that I pick up some of the people going from this side of the district. So . . . you and Johnny will be going with me!'

'Oh, no, we won't!' The words came out loudly, emphatically, but then she smiled carefully as she saw her brother swing round in his seat to glance quickly at them. He asked uncertainly, beginning to stand up, 'What is it, Sis?'

Then he saw that Dominic was laughing and it was their visitor who answered him. 'We were only discussing that young farmers' outing, Johnny. Everyone seems to have a different opinion as to which farm we should visit. Your sister, for one!'

'Oh, is that all?' The boy returned to his programme. Wherever they went was all right with him. One could always learn something from any farm . . . even if he knew that this time it wouldn't be a tobacco one.

A small, satisfied smile curved Dominic's lips as he glanced from his turned back to the girl sitting at the table. 'There you are,' he said. 'I'll see you then. But for now I'd better be off. I have a meeting, and then I'm going away for a fortnight or so, but I'll be back in time for that affair. So long.' He raised a hand in a small half-wave, said goodnight to her brother, and was gone.

Letitia watched his figure until it ran down the back veranda steps and turned a corner. She put both arms around her chest, hugging herself as if she were cold, then with an effort she rose from the table, quickly cleared it, washed up, then said to the figure engrossed in the television, 'I'm off to bed—goodnight.'

Showering away tiredness from the long day of

driving and in her shortie nightdress, she picked up her hairbrush and went to stand by the window.

But as she brushed her silver-gilt hair with long, soothing strokes, she thought of Dominic. Last night, with so much heartburning, she had made her resolutions. Now, with just one appearance, he had smashed them all to pieces.

He had come as if on an ordinary, neighbourly visit; and only once had that attitude changed—when his expression had taken on that glinting pirate's look, while glancing from her to the teapot, and telling her he wouldn't dare take his clothes home ruined. She was aware it had been only kindness that had made him come tonight. He would know, experienced man-about-town that he was, how she would feel after that passionate lovemaking, and then his abrupt abandoning of her.

So if he was going to be away for a fortnight, and he must be, it was to let her know that that was the reason for his absence; not the one she would inevitably jump to, and feel so chagrined about.

He was just being kind, she decided again. He hadn't meant to make love to her as he had done last night, and this evening's visit was to try to get their acquaintanceship back on a friendly basis. After all, if it wasn't, Mareeba was much too small a town for it not to be noticed.

But oh——! Letitia's eyes closed tightly, and she was abruptly looking into other eyes, feeling lips come down so warmly on hers. Her entire body gave a deep shudder, and she knew that in any sort of way, whatever he wanted, Dominic would only have to say, Come with me, Letitia, and she would go.

Abruptly she swung around. There was no use thinking these sort of thoughts. She would meet him as he wanted, casually and friendly—and then keep as far away from him as she could. She switched out the overhead light, put on the bedside one, and banked the pillows up behind her back. She had a good book which had been lying there waiting to be read, so she began to read it.

It was no good. The printed words ran into one another. Impatiently she closed it and switched out the light. She knew she wouldn't get to sleep, but it was no good trying to read when vivid emerald-green eyes smiled out at her from the pages; and they were still looking quizzically at her when, in nature's way of taking care of its own, she went fathoms deep into sleep.

CHAPTER SIX

AND so the next fortnight passed. Letitia was learning to dismiss Dominic from her thoughts for most of the daytime—the night hours were a different matter altogether.

The Tuesday and Wednesday after the shopping foray in Cairns and Dominic's brief visit the same night, she worked among her mangoes. And when once the thought of the handsome man did intrude, her smile turned to acid. Why hadn't he first seen her like this; then there probably would never have been any involvement.

He wouldn't have looked twice at her, accepting her as just some woman working in the field, although possibly he would have cast a second look her way, because she wasn't in shorts and a loose top, which was the normal working gear up here in the north. She wore jeans tucked into wellingtons, a long-sleeved shirt, gardening gloves, hair pushed under a large hat, and over her face, the only skin showing, a deep covering of apricot oil.

Peter, arriving out here once on a departmental visit, had stared, then laughed like a fool. All he received in return was a complacent grin. Some girls, especially those going to the coast a lot, tanned themselves brown and black, and Letitia acknowledged that they looked wonderful. But she just shrugged. Each to her own. She loved the climate up here, but with her fair skin she didn't want too much scorching sunshine on it.

But Thursday was different. Thursday she went into town and had a game of tennis at the Club. She enjoyed it, because it kept her thoughts away from something she didn't want to think about. Then she did the household shopping, and as she was stacking the packages into the boot of the car, a voice behind her said, 'Hello there, Letitia.'

She turned to see Rosa smiling at her, so she said, returning it in kind, 'Oh, hello, have you been shopping too?'

'Yes. I was wondering, have you finished, Letitia?' Rosa was asking.

'Yes, I'm on my way home now, Rosa. How are you?'

'Oh, I'm fine. However, Dominic was telling me you wanted a piece of my *dama de notte*.'

'I certainly do, if you could spare it. I fell in love with the perfume the other night.'

'Well, why don't you follow me now, and I'll give you a clipping. Actually, though, it will be more than that, as I have a nice piece potted.'

Letitia hesitated, her first quick thought being one of refusal. That place belonged to Dominic . . . Still, he wasn't there—and she would be going to the manager's house.

So she said, 'Right, I'll do that, Rosa, and thanks.'

Following the small blue shining car in front, Letitia wondered what make it was, thinking of the secret she was going to impart with such glee to her brother when she got home.

However, her thoughts slid away from these reflections as she reached the private driveway. Passing it, she allowed herself only one swift sideways glance at the beautiful white villa, seeing as she did so sprinklers busily shedding moisture on the great expanse of velvety green lawn on which it sat. Dominic might be away, but the working life of the place went on just the same.

Pulling up behind Rosa, she saw that there was a

lawn here too, albeit only a small one. Rosa told her as she stepped from the car, 'It's around the back,' and set off along a small path.

But, arriving around the back Letitia stopped sharply with a small gasp of delight. The whole place was a riot of colour, flower beds and trees laid out carefully, and some distance away was a wide trellis covered with the brilliance of royal purple. The bougainvillaea was in bloom. Letitia knew that up here bougainvillaea was a common plant, but when in flower, it was a delight. She said as much.

'Yes, I agree. I love looking out of my back window and seeing all that colour,' answered her companion. 'But of course it has no scent at all! That's why I have a supplementary trellis at either end, one for my sweet peas and one for my jasmine. And of course, I have my *dama de notte.*' Rosa laughed as she added, 'You know that when we moved here into what was then called the big house after Dominic's father died, I had those trellises planted to hide the big farm buildings. I realise they're necessary, but they're not pretty—not like my trellises of flowers, are they?'

Letitia gave an answering laugh, saying, 'I think you're absolutely right, Rosa. But don't let anyone else hear us talking like this.'

'No, I certainly won't,' said Rosa, smiling, 'but look, here we are.' She bent down to pick up a rather big pot with a healthy-looking bush growing in it. 'I'll just put this in your boot,' she said. 'And you get Mario to plant it for you, remember. He knows how.'

'Yes, I will, and thanks, Rosa.' Driving away, Letitia had leisure now to give more than a passing glance at this beautiful home of Dominic's as she went by it. She shrugged, and a wave of melancholy overcame her. She wished suddenly that she had never met him. She had been quite happy in her own life before.

The days passed, and she went about her normal way

of living. She worked among her mango trees; she helped Johnny and Mario when she could. She just let the hours and days pass over her. And then, on the Monday before the Cairns weekend, Johnny found trouble among his tobacco. Peter was out in the paddocks for hours before leaving to check with head office. Mario went for Giovanni, and then he too left to check with others.

Letitia took both lunch and dinner over to the farm buildings, then, unable to help the two anxious men, returned to the farmhouse. She almost jumped out of her skin when Johnny came bursting in later that evening while she was watching television.

He said breathlessly, 'We're going to try to find Peter . . . or Giovanni if we can't get him. We think we know what's the matter. You needn't wait up for me, I might be quite a while. 'Night!' He was gone.

Letitia sighed. At least he sounded pleased, so it could be all right after all. She looked at the film she had been watching, but decided she wouldn't bother, so switched it off. She closed the big glass doors, but left the light on for her brother.

At least she was tired. She had made it her business to make herself tired every day, but she was reading, pillows stacked behind her back, when she heard the car return and drive over to the farm buildings. And she was still engrossed in her book when a voice called to her from the back veranda. A frown between her brows, she got out of bed and threw a soft lace housecoat over her short nightdress.

Only half opening the door, she saw Peter, and was beginning to tell him that Johnny wasn't at home, when she was interrupted. 'Sorry, Letitia . . . I know they aren't here, but the stupid clots left a roll of barbed wire, and a rusty one at that, right in front of the bulk-shed— and I fell into it. My leg seems to be bleeding rather freely. Do you think I might see to it?'

'Of course,' she told him, pulling him inside, and then saw his face . . . and the leg of his trousers. 'Good heavens,' she exclaimed, horrified. 'Quick, come into the bathroom.'

One leg of his long khaki trousers was torn in several places, and blood was spreading in big patches. Letitia said baldly, 'Can I cut your trouser leg?'

'I expect you'd better. It wouldn't look too good if I was found here in my underpants, now would it?' Peter was laughing. But to Letitia this was no laughing matter. She was frightened. She got a pair of sharp scissors and slit downwards.

'Oh, Peter!' she exclaimed again. 'There's one big gash and several deep jagged holes where the barbs must have caught you. Look,' her hurried voice told him, 'I'll clean it with antiseptic, and try to stop that bleeding, then you're going straight to a doctor.' She got busy then, and later, as she pulled tightly on a gauze dressing, Peter began to lose his balance.

'Look out!' he cried, and grabbed her. Hanging on to one another, they were suddenly laughing out loud, the tension still there, but easing.

Letitia told him, 'For heaven's sake, Peter, keep still. I've got to get this fastened.'

'Don't you think I'm trying to keep as still as I can? *You* just try standing on one leg like a stork, and we'll see how you go. Oh, lord—look, I've got blood all over you . . . all over your nightdress!'

Letitia waved away such unimportant matters. 'Pooh,' she said. 'What does a little blood matter? What does matter is to go and get it attended to properly, and most likely get a tetanus booster.'

'I expect I'd better, at that. But I'll have to go to Outpatients at the hospital. I won't find any doctor at this hour.'

'Oh yes, you will find a doctor—mine. You're going to no hospital. That dashed barbed wire is our fault.

And I don't want any repercussions later if anything happens to you.'

'Thank you very much for having me dying already!' Peter was laughing again, and Letitia looked at the face so close to her own, felt the arm around her for stability tighten, saw his expression. She told him, laughing herself now, 'Oh, no, you don't, Peter. You're a wounded man. A doctor and bed is all you're fit for tonight.'

'And I expect you're right at that,' he said, then added, 'I'm really all right now, though.'

'I'm glad of that, because I'm not very up in nursing. I don't know whether to give you a brandy or not. But sit here for a minute. I'm going to ring my doctor.'

It was only the minute or so specified, when she returned, saying, 'No, no alcohol. But you're to go to Dr Elder. He's waiting for you now at home and will treat you there. You'd better get there at once, Peter. I'm very worried about that leg! Now, can you drive?' she was adding anxiously. 'I don't think I could manage your utility, and as you know, Johnny isn't here.'

Peter stood up. He looked down at his flapping trouser leg, then laughed, saying, 'Don't be silly, Letitia. I've played inter-varsity football, I've had far worse than this happen to me.'

But she only shook her head, and went with him as far as the veranda. She told him warmly, 'Please drive carefully, Peter. I'll see you tomorrow.'

He raised a hand in a half-wave and walked off, not even limping. She waited until she heard the truck start, then made her way to the bathroom.

Shrugging off the darkly stained nightdress, she got back into the thin lace housecoat, buttoning up only two buttons, intending to get into something fresh as soon as she had cleared up here. She did that, then washed her hands thoroughly with scented soap. Then, walking out of there to go to her bedroom, she halted blindly, her heart jolting.

She couldn't speak for a moment as the two silent, immobile figures stood gazing directly at one another. Then she managed, her voice sounding strange even to her own ears, 'Dominic . . . what are you doing here? I didn't hear you knock!'

'Oh, I thought it might possibly be open house here tonight. That as you were so forthcoming . . .' An eyebrow almost went up to his hairline as he left that enigmatic sentence remain unfinished.

Pulling the thin lace négligé as closely about her as she could manage, Letitia didn't answer for a moment, almost frightened by the different way that familiar face looked. She said again, 'What are you doing here, Dominic? And I wouldn't expect you to walk straight in without knocking.'

'To answer your question as to what I'm doing here— well, I did come on an altogether different matter from the one I'm now contemplating . . . which is to continue with that unfinished business we started the other night.'

She had thought at times, when Dominic showed that glinting, wicked look, that he took on the appearance of a swashbuckling pirate. But it had always been only a laughing pirate. Not like tonight! Tonight only a grim ruthlessness showed in both speech and manner.

'You mustn't be bashful,' he was continuing in that soft, silken, frightening tone, 'and try to fasten up that flimsy thing you have one. I don't expect it was between you and Madison, so why should it come between us? Also you should understand, my dear Letitia, that if you want to make love in a lighted bathroom, instead of in the privacy of your bedroom, you take the chance that any passing stranger could observe the spectacle. But we shan't make that mistake, shall we?'

Hearing those words, utterly unable to take in the meaning they carried, her mind reeling in disbelief at such a tone, Letitia said curtly, 'You're drunk, Dominic! Go home!'

'Oh no, I'm not drunk! I only wish I were! Then I'd wake up tomorrow realising it was all a bad dream, and really, Letitia . . .' The man reached over so lazily—it was like a slow-motion picture—and with one hand gripped firmly on the neck of the gown she had been holding tightly clasped about her, he pulled.

The fragile material which held the button fastenings ripped, the two sides falling apart. Letitia tried to hold them together over her naked form. She was suddenly too angry to be frightened; if she could have killed him, she would have.

She said furiously, 'You barbarian! Get out of here or I'm calling the police, and you'd better not be here when they come!' She was speaking with the same acid softness that he had been using.

The three steps she took to the phone were over-taken. She didn't hear his footsteps, they were stalking like some jungle predator, and she was caught and swung up into corded arms. Struggling, furious, she found herself carried to her bedroom with the same silent tread, the door kicked shut, and on the bed, she found herself held prisoner with an arm planted firmly on either side.

'I've shut the door,' came that soft, absolutely unknown, hateful voice. 'We don't want any interruptions, now, do we? Unless of course Johnny agrees with your behaviour, and aids and abets it.'

Letitia had read about white-hot rage—she had never thought to experience it. She said between clenched teeth, Get out of my home, Dominic Catalano. How I ever thought you could even be a friend is beyond me . . .'

She broke off, because Dominic was saying, 'Oh no, not a friend,' he smiled down at her with thinned lips, 'Oh, no,' he repeated, 'there's no friendship involved now. I'm going to make love to you—make love in my own fashion, completely. Afterwards . . . Oh, well, you can think of Madison afterwards. But I'll guarantee that for a time you'll forget him. I do have the reputation among my . . . women friends, of being quite competent, you know.'

Beginning to be frightened in earnest, she began to tell him the reason why Peter had been here; but his lips came down on hers as she opened them to explain. She went rigid, her whole body rebelling.

Then those seeking lips lifted, and Dominic spoke, his tone as softly silken as before. 'Oh, do you think, my promiscuous but so innocent-looking maiden, that you're not going to respond to me? You are, you know! Don't you remember another time in this house . . . you responded then. Then, I could have done whatever I wanted to, without any repulsion at all . . . Oh, no!' the last two words were ejaculated as she writhed, trying to get away, knowing that what he was saying had been true . . . then.

There came one swift fluid movement, and his long heavy body was lying beside her own, crushing one arm beneath him, her other arm clasped tightly by the wrist.

Leaning over her, his face intent, lids covering eyes which showed only slits to see through, he said, 'I'm going to make love to you properly, because that's all I've been thinking of this past fortnight, then I hope you'll be out of my system. Do you realise I didn't go on the other night because I thought you were too young, too innocent, to know what consequences some lovemaking could bring? What a fool I was!' A low contemptuous laugh sounded. 'How stupid could I have been? Has Madison been your lover all along?' He was speaking to her between little kisses he was placing along her exposed throat like beads in a necklace, 'And then the other night, when you would have fallen so effortlessly into my arms, did you think that I with all my wealth—and I have a very great deal, my dear Letitia—would be the better catch?

'I expect you also don't know that for the first time in my life I was serious about a woman. Too bad for you that I had to walk past that window such a short time ago and see you both locked into each other's arms, laughing, looking into one another's eyes with remembrance. Will you say to me, my dear Letitia, when I finally go, "Do drive carefully, Dominic. I'll see you tomorrow!"

'But I'm afraid, my free and easy girl of today's world, that tonight is all you'll be seeing of me. Tomorrow you'll just be someone I'll have to nod to when not doing so would cause comment. But oh, tonight . . .!' He was kissing her lips now, deep, slow, heartbreaking kisses. She wasn't going to respond . . . she wasn't. She was too angry that he could think the thoughts he did about her.

And then without conscious will, without volition on her own part her body jumped. Dominic's long warm fingers had trailed along her bare skin, over her breasts, to come to rest spreadeagled in the hollow of her hips.

She felt his hand there, not warm now, but scorching its mark on the nerves of her entire body. She said faintly, 'Dominic, don't!' But the only answer she received was that soft laughter from way back in his throat.

And then she couldn't prevent her traitorous self from responding as she felt his lips scorching their way along that trail his fingers had already broken. Nerve-ends flaring, her body twisted.

'Oh, yes,' he was murmuring, his head lifting a little from what he was doing, 'It's too late to turn back now.

Too late to say, "Don't, Dominic." And do you know, a few minutes ago, all I was interested in was revenge for my stupidity . . . for, what's the modern idiom for it, being taken for a ride. But now I find I'm beginning to enjoy it.'

Letitia tried to move a leg and kick, and his heavy limb was thrown across her body to suppress the movement. Then he had risen a little, and with the one hand not holding her had begun to undo buttons and clasps.

She wasn't going to cry, she decided, blinking furiously. But she would hate him for always . . . she knew it was too late for entreaties. He would only laugh again. She said bleakly, 'I wonder what your cousins would think if they could see this . . . and you!' Scorn echoed in her voice.

'But my dear Letitia, my cousins would never be in this sort of a situation. They're looked after more carefully.'

'Oh, of course. But aren't they lucky that they didn't have a grandfather dying just a few weeks ago, a father shot down in the service of his country, and a young brother out trying to save his crop? Oh, lucky them, that they also didn't have an Australian barbarian breaking into their home, to do what an Italian barbarian is doing now!'

The long form holding her down, the hand scorching her bare skin, the mouth that had been plundering its way all over her, were abruptly still, rigid. Then the long warm body was no longer there. It had rolled off the bed and was standing upright beside it.

And, just as suddenly, Letitia was standing on its other side, the bed a barrier between them. With her crumpled, ripped gown clutched tightly about her, her dishevelled silver-gilt hair tumbling around her face, her lips burning a deeply vivid crimson from his kisses, she gazed across at him.

Almost as dishevelled as she herself was; for the first

time she saw his dark hair rumpled, falling all over his forehead, his clothing not immaculate as she had always known it . . . and his eyes for once wide open.

His hand went up palm outward in the peace gesture she had seen it once make to Johnny. 'I apologise for my behaviour,' said that strange, unknown voice of tonight, then it added, 'Of course you have the right to act as you want to—and with whom you want to. I'll never bother you again—and I'll never come here again either!'

His glance flashed once more over her, then he had turned and was gone. And like another time, Letitia stood still, immobile, waiting to hear the Jaguar start up and drive away. She didn't hear it.

Then slowly she slid down by the bed, and on the floor put her head down low. He wasn't going to make her faint, either—nor cry. Then the world and reality about her returned. She pulled herself up with the aid of the bed, and with slow, creaking footsteps walked to the bathroom.

She turned the shower on full, and scrubbed herself all over. Then, out and wrapped in a large bath-towel, she found a plastic garbage bag to ease within it the nightdress stained with Peter's blood, and the ripped and crumpled négligé. She never wanted to see either again. Both would go into the incinerator tomorow.

Tiredly, she returned to her room and with her hair still wet crept into bed. She knew she would have to face up to the happenings of tonight some time—but not tonight! Tonight she felt only desolation, loss . . .

CHAPTER SEVEN

LETITIA slid out of the back seat, smiling a thank-you to Peter as he handed over her case. She moved to the front seat of the car and leaned over him to speak to her brother. 'You drive carefully now, Johnny,' she told him.

'Oh, come on, Sis, you say that every time. Of course I will; but wouldn't it have been beaut if your new car had arrived, instead of getting here next week? It would have been just the thing for this trip!'

'Yes, my love, wouldn't it have been?' answered Letitia with a grave face, and turned quickly away from the sardonic grin Peter was directing at her. She wasn't at all sorry that the new car hadn't arrived. She would rather her brother didn't begin to drive it while going down winding, precipitous roads. But he would have been very indignant if she had told him so.

'Oh, there's Dominic!' cried Johnny, as the long grey car slid past. It drew in just ahead and a tall figure in the immaculate clothes it always wore stepped from it. Dominic walked round the bonnet, turning to lean into the offside window.

Letitia had made it her business to arrange carefully that she went in other transport this weekend, so now she turned casually away until her back was to both man and car. She told her brother, 'Look, although I'm staying with the Kellys at the motel, I'll see you at the farms and at the dinner, so don't go having too wild a time with it at your billet. However, I really am sorry about you being unable to play host, Peter, and I hate seeing you still limping. You have my heartfelt permission to take it all out on Johnny for being so careless.'

'No worries, Letitia. I'm really going to enjoy today. And being looked after will be quite a change.'

'OK, I'll see you there, then.' She laughed in at him, and received an answering laugh. Just good friends, it had apparently been decided now, she thought thankfully as she waved the vehicle off. She didn't see the man standing by the Jaguar's open door glance swiftly their way as he heard the burst of merriment, then just as quickly look away.

She *did* hear Johnny honk the horn as he passed Dominic's car, and she saw a cashmere-clad arm wave back. She also wondered acidly if this was one of the times he felt he had to wave; just as he would have to nod at a girl when ignoring her would cause comment.

She turned to get into the car which had just pulled into the kerb, and stepped into the back seat. 'Hi there, Marge . . . and Les,' she greeted the two in the front. The woman turned with her arm lying across the headrest as her husband followed the big grey car driving off ahead of them.

The talk was of farming, of course. And especially of the one they were going to see this afternoon; the consensus being that it would be great to see this new experimental farm which Dominic Catalano had arranged to have opened to them. Letitia only listened, answering with just an occasional murmur. This was how she was made aware of anything about him now— listening to other people's talk.

She settled back as they started down the range road, the view a good excuse for her silence. Seeing Dominic just now had brought back that dreadful night she was determined not to think of. She had heard Johnny come in and shower. She had lain feeling the hours of the night pass over her. She had also known she would have to come to terms with what had happened if she was going to stay here these next six months for Johnny's sake.

But most of all she had wondered why. And as she remembered, actual nausea had overtaken her. She had turned, burying her face in the pillow.

No one . . . no man . . . had ever behaved remotely to her as Dominic had done. Why? Again the wonder came. She simply couldn't understand it! Because anyone would have thought that Dominic Catalano, seeing what he had thought he had seen, would shrug his shoulders and walk away. With all that he had going for him, his wealth, his looks, the charisma that hung about him, he would never be short of willing partners in anything he proposed.

But, thinking of that other time he had made love to her, she knew that, completed or not, she would still have been in love with him afterwards . . . because even that flaming desire and passion had carried with it a hint of protective caring.

But tonight . . .! Well, she had thought about it and now she was going to forget it. There was one thing about that assured, ruthless man, he only said what he meant. He wouldn't be bothering her again.

Then later, still unable to sleep, she slipped quietly from her bed, and in the bathroom shook two white tablets from the aspirin bottle, then, shrugging, added a third. She swallowed the small pills down with water. There, that should help her sleep. But oblivion took its time in coming.

Next morning she overslept. Startled by the blazing sunlight coming through the window, she automatically lifted her wrist. Almost ten o'clock, and silence reigned all through the house. Johnny must have gone over to the paddocks without waking her.

As she swung her legs over the side of the bed, suddenly realisation hit at her, and her body stopped dead. Then her shoulders straightened, she drew jeans off a hanger, and with a long-sleeved shirt dressed swiftly. She wanted no great areas of exposed flesh showing today.

Outside, she shaded her eyes and gazed across to the farm buildings. Johnny called to her from among the tobacco. He came out from the small green bushes and crossed over to her. 'We had fun and games yesterday, didn't we! But we found the trouble, and Giovanni gave us some spray. Everything is OK now, Sis, but gee, didn't I panic yesterday?'

'Yes, everything is OK if you fixed it up,' Letitia agreed wryly, 'so I'll let you get on with it.' She went to turn away.

Johnny spoke quickly. 'You look a bit pale, Letitia. You aren't ill, are you?' And suddenly, anxiety clouded the young voice.

'Of course I'm not ill,' she answered, dredging up a smile for him. 'Well, maybe I caught a touch of that virus that's going around.'

'Look, I'll eat my lunch over here. Go and take some aspirins and go back to bed. You have that farmers' do this weekend, you know. You have to be better for that,' said her brother.

'Oh, yes,' she told herself, returning to the house. She had to be fit for that. And she dashed well would be! But she wouldn't be taking any more aspirins, thank you very much. Today was another day.

She squeezed some oranges and, taking up the glass, walked to the phone. 'Carol,' she replied to the answering voice, 'would you please ask Dr Elder if Peter Madison got his tetanus booster last night?' She listened, said, 'Thank you,' and returned the receiver to its cradle. Well, that was that. The loose ends of last night were tied. It was finished!

She made herself tea and toast—and didn't want it. Outside, in a long lounging chair set under a big shady tree, she lay gazing up through the tracery of leaves at a lapis-lazuli sky. She went to sleep.

Speaking across to her for the second time, Marge's voice brought her out of those unhappy recollections and back to the present with a start. 'Yes, I see,' she answered, and she did see. Clouds were beginning to pile up one on top of the other. As Marge had called across to her, it did look as if it might rain. Oh well, you took what the Lord provided.

The winding range road was behind them now, and they were turning north from the town. There was no trouble with finding their destination. Cars they know were travelling both before and after them. They parked where they were directed and then stepped out to see what was to be seen.

'For as far as you can see, those are avocado trees,' said a voice behind them, and as the Kellys started off, Letitia turned to the smiling young man she had met that day in Cairns.

'I'll tell you all about them in a moment,' he was adding, 'but first I'm booking my dance for tonight. OK?'

Glancing around the milling crowd scattered about, with more than a few very attractive young girls among it, Letitia laughed. 'I think I should be the one to get in and grab,' she replied, and added, 'Yes, thank you, Richard. One dance, I think you said.' Then as he went to continue, she changed the subject.

'Look, Richard, we have two avocado trees at home. And allow me to inform you, they're not like these bushes.'

'Of course, and they bear big fruit too, which are beauties, but these are a different variety. You know, once upon a time we—Australians, I mean—didn't eat avocados much. But now they're on every restaurant menu; and people buy them to spread on bread and butter. Hence this big farm, owned by a company down south.' Richard turned as his name was called, shrugged and said, 'My master's voice—I have to be off, but I'll see you later.'

Letitia followed in his footsteps, listened as they were all doing, but didn't ask questions as they were all doing; her subconscious aware always of a tall figure strolling with other figures who weren't farmers.

Then she found Peter beside her. He had his arm around an attractive honey-blonde. Letitia smiled happily at him, and, reading her expression, he grinned back. 'Well,' he told her softly, 'crying for the moon isn't a sensible thing to do, they tell me, so . . .'

'You never cried for any moon,' she answered him just as softly, thankful for the crush that had just come to swirl around them. And it was also with thankfulness that she smiled lovingly at him as she would have done at Johnny.

And again, as on the morning up in Mareeba, she didn't see a man notice that smiling scene, and again, that he turned just as quickly away.

But Peter was saying, 'I've been looking for you, Letitia. Come and see what I've found out. It's just the thing for you.' Mystified, she went, and among the spreading young trees Peter leant down and turned a small nozzle. Nothing seemed to happen, and she frowned at him as he continued to smile happily, his arm still clasped around his blonde.

He said, 'Look down and feel.'

Exasperated, Letitia felt like walking away; but this was Peter, and this environment was his job. So she did as instructed. She bent down and felt. The soil all around was wet.

'It's called trickle irrigation, Letitia. Dominic is interested in it. You know when you irrigate up home, the water sprays upwards in a vast waterfall. That's what's needed for tobacco bushes. But this new idea would suit your mangoes much better, and look how it would save on your water bill!'

'Yes, indeed it would,' she answered, as they all turned away, Peter and his companion wandering off. So she stood alone, arms hugged tightly about her, searching the crowd for the Kellys. The clouds were coming even lower, a few spots of rain falling, and she felt cold. Their winter, even if it was mild, was beginning to appear. She had been silly to leave her cardigan in the car.

A presence had materialised behind her as she stood still scanning the throng, and a cool, impersonal voice said, 'Put this on, it's getting cold, and it could rain.'

Unable to even try to answer that unexpected voice for a long second, she then managed, 'Go away, please,' and remained rigid, her arms still clasped about her.

A seeming mountain of softness fell around her shoulders and Dominic said, 'It's quite new, and if you take it off and throw it on the ground, you'll look very silly.' He was walking away.

Letitia remained rooted to the spot, the soft cashmere jumper enclosing her. She gazed swiftly around. No one was watching; no one was interested. Everyone had other subjects to occupy their attention.

She felt sick. There was no doubt she was already feeling the warmth of the covering about her. But she wanted it off—and she really couldn't understand why Dominic had done what he had done . . . after the other night.

So carefully she withdrew her hands from beneath the enveloping folds and shrugged the garment from her shoulders. Thankfully she noticed then that there was a move towards inside, and afternoon tea. So she left it folded neatly on a chair-back where it would be seen by its owner.

She lost herself among a young group, and accepted the plate of avocado-spread biscuits and the cup of tea which Richard found for her. She drank the tea, but she hid the plate and its contents. And not long afterwards she was grateful when Marge found her and said, 'Look, Letitia, there's not much more to see today, and I think it's really going to rain. So do you want to come to the motel with us now, or stay and watch the rest?'

'Oh, no . . . I mean, oh, yes, please,' she answered, then smiled as Marge laughed. 'I meant,' she elucidated, 'that yes, please, I want to come back with you.'

She waved to her brother as she went past, and looked completely through some businessmen who were still being shown around, especially through the very tall one who was now wearing a grey cashmere jumper. She collapsed tiredly into the back seat of Les's car.

And, still later, she swung round before the mirror, endeavouring to take in her reflection as a whole, and thought, 'I do look all right.' And she did! But it had taken a long, hot shower, and then a cold one, before that hazy, clouded feeling was swirled away.

Now she glanced at her eye make-up, with which she had used a generous hand, and decided again that the green shadow did match her buttons and belt. And, pointing out one shoe, she decided also that its jade green completed the overall picture.

Picking up her small evening purse, she turned away from the dressing table, silver-gilt hair swinging on her shoulders, tangerine silk frothing about her knees as she moved and went outside.

Les was standing by the car. Letitia pulled shut her door and walked across to him. He said, 'Good heavens, Letitia! I wouldn't have known you . . . and I've known you since you were a very small schoolgirl taking tennis lessons. Tonight you look like a model from one of those glossy magazines.'

With a gurgle of laughter, Letitia asked, 'Truly?'

'Truly?' he mimicked her, and his wife, joining them, said, 'What's truly?' then added before he could reply, 'Oh, Letitia, you do look nice.'

'That's what I was just telling her. And so do you, my dear.'

Letitia gurgled again with laughter, saying as she stepped into the back seat of the car, 'Flattery will get you everywhere, Les. You'll get on.'

However, walking into the big hall with its flower-decked tables, its crowd of familiar faces even if they were in unfamiliar clothes, she didn't feel easy and carefree. Her body was tense, and she knew her glance was searching for one particular figure—hoping it might not be present. But then her nerves contracted. It was! And Dominic had turned and was looking at her—although for only the briefest second. Then he had swung away and only his profile was turned towards her.

She made herself take a deep breath. She *had* thought she looked attractive in her new, lovely, expensive dress. But Dominic! He was something to make every woman in the hall look . . . and think of Roman gods and high romance. She drew in a second deep breath, while deciding that that was not so with her. She allowed her glance to swing wide.

But in those narrow black trousers, that pristine white dinner jacket, which showed off so starkly the brown, handsome face, he was a figure that dreams were made of.

Standing with the Kellys, she smiled and spoke to the people around her that she knew, but then she said, 'I don't think I belong among this senior and rarefied atmosphere, will you all excuse me while I go across to where I really belong?' She felt she couldn't stay any longer in this small group containing Dominic.

Nice, kind James Fenton said, 'Of course—I'll personally escort to where you'll probably enjoy yourself more.' And, taking hold of her arm, he did just that, delivering her over to Richard, who grinned and said, 'To whom do I give thanks for this beauty bestowed upon me? The fates . . . or just Lady Luck?' Peter also smiled at her from beside his blonde. And . . . Her eyebrows climbed.

She found herself looking at a brother who was more tidily dressed than she had ever seen him. And he was beaming at a petite dark girl. Unaware of doing so, Letitia looked her over, then caught herself up, smiling at her own behaviour.

Johnny walked the few steps to her side. He said, 'Hi, there, Sis. I didn't catch up with you this afternoon. Did Dominic show you that new trickle irrigation?'

Ignoring his question, she smiled up at him and said, 'Hello, handsome, you seem to be doing all right,' and laughed as he moved hurriedly away with only a grin for answer.

The gavel banged for them to take their seats. The speeches were short and witty, the called-out replies bringing laughter. These few minutes set the tone for the evening—for an evening that was happy and gay. Letitia kept her attention among her own group, about her own table, as waiters began filling glasses and bringing food, and found in this way that she was really beginning to enjoy this first time at a dinner after a field farm day.

The meal finished, the dancing started, and Letitia found out something she hadn't expected. She found she was no wallflower. Peter wasn't dancing, and she asked him a little anxiously, 'Is your leg really all right, Peter? It's not like you not to be dancing.'

He gave her a wide smile as he told her, 'I only had the stitches out yesterday and was ordered to be a bit careful. So I'm playing the wounded hero. I don't expect,' here he held out a hand to her, 'you'd like to take pity on a wounded hero, would you?'

'Oh, I might, on a wounded hero,' she laughed back

at him. 'But you're not wounded now. And you've had more than your share of the fair sex dancing attendance on you today!' She waved to him as she went off to dance.

And it was later, just before the evening would be ending, that the shock came. As a form paused before her, she glanced up to smile—and froze.

'Will you dance this with me, Letitia?' asked the familiar soft voice.

Wildly she looked about her, but the chairs in the immediate vicinity were empty. She said breathlessly, 'Please go away, Dominic. You have no right to harass me like this. You know I won't dance with you.'

'Well, I'm afraid you're going to have to—or cause a scene. Because I want to talk to you.'

'But I don't want to talk to you! Just go away!'

'I still want to ask you a question, Letitia. And I'm going to.'

'Very well, Dominic. If you touch me . . . if you try to dance with me,' she told him, her glance fixed over his shoulder, before bringing it back to meet his gaze, 'if you put your arm around me, I'd probably be sick all over you . . . and then it would be *you* having to burn your clothes in an incinerator tomorrow.' The words reached out to him, hard, and carrying no friendliness at all.

He couldn't be said to go pale with that dark skin, but his colour did change. His face closed up and he said, 'Very well, you've made your point. Now I'm going to make mine! We won't dance. However . . .' the words came out more flatly than hers had done, ice-cold, 'I will come and fetch you to escort you home. Make no mistake about that, Letitia! If you want to have the whole hall looking on at a scene—be my guest. I don't care about any disturbance I'm involved in. My reputation will take anything it has to, because I simply don't give a damn.

'Still, for you it's different. I'll collect you at the beginning of the last dance. I want a question answered!' He had turned and had strolled off, for all the world like a man who had just been having a few pleasant words with an attractive girl.

'I won't,' she muttered fiercely to herself. 'I'm not going with him!' But suddenly she wasn't muttering. A memory had struck at her. What was the question he wanted answered? Recollecting the way he had walked off and the words he had used just now, and especially remembering how he had declared after that dreadful night that he would never bother her again, this new overture was not in keeping with the assured, arrogant man that Dominic was . . .

She laughed away the last half-hour, and wondered how she could force herself to do it. Then the music started and Dominic was standing before her.

He didn't take her elbow. He walked beside her like an elderly uncle escorting home a niece from an outing. He did throw up a hand, laughing, at one shouted comment coming their way, and Letitia felt her cheeks go hot. Determinedly, looking everywhere but at her companion, she suddenly saw a woman rising to dance. With a hand on her partner's shoulder, she allowed her glance to rove all over Dominic, then return it to his face.

There was no prize for guessing what she was thinking; it showed openly in her countenance for all to read. Dominic might conjure up such feelings in the opposite sex, with the way he was, with that charismatic assured arrogance that was a part of him, but, Letitia thought furiously, you can have him with my compliments!

Then they had walked past, and outside she felt the ocean breeze cool her hot cheeks. She also felt the rain. Her companion said, 'Wait here. I'll bring the car across. It would be a pity to get that beautiful dress wet.'

She swung round to him, wondering if he was being sarcastic, but he had already left for the car park, apparently not caring if his tuxedo and dress trousers got wet.

Almost immediately the Jaguar was driving into the kerb beside her, and its driver had leaned over to open the door. She stepped in and began to speak. Dominic told her, 'Later, Letitia,' then added, 'Fasten your seat-belt.'

She fastened it, hating that bleak, ice-cold tone he was using, and her teeth clenched tightly. But she only said, gazing out through the rain-streaked windows, 'This isn't the way to my motel.'

'No, it is not! And I'm not abducting you. I just want a straight answer to one question, and then we'll go on from there.'

'Look, it doesn't matter what question you want to ask, or what answer you expect to get. All that's not relevant now. I really don't want anything to do with you, Dominic. I don't even want to be near you again!'

Only silence answered her.

They left the rain-filled night behind as Dominic drove into an underground car park. He stepped out and came round to open her door. He moved back, making no attempt to help her out.

Unwillingly, Letitia eased off her seat-belt and joined him on the cement floor. He said, 'We have to walk up two flights of stairs. There's no lift, as the owners opted for privacy.' He finished speaking and stood aside at the beginning of the steps.

At the top was a heavy door, like the solid wooden one in his home at Mareeba. He unlocked it.

A switch clicked and the door shut behind them. Letitia glanced about her. The owner of this unit might want privacy, but it wasn't furnished with luxurious divans or brilliant colours. It was almost an austere room. A maroon carpet, deeply soft to walk upon, met cool ivory walls. Then she heard another click behind her. Dominic had pressed a button on a console, and with a swish, maroon curtains slid shut across what must be an entire wall of glass.

For the rest, there were a couple of carved chests, some similar small coffee tables, and at the far end, a small dining-room setting.

Not again! she thought angrily. He's not being fair to start this all over again. He promised . . . he did!

CHAPTER EIGHT

LETITIA stood rigidly still as he came across to face her. 'I expect,' he said, 'it's of no use asking you to sit down, is it?'

Receiving no reply, he tightened his lips, and she made herself shake her head.

'Very well. Then tell me, please, precisely what happened that Monday night?'

Outraged, eyes wide, she stared furiously back at him. 'Are you mad? How can you even ask?' she almost spat.

'I mean before I came on the scene.'

She took a couple of steps backwards and said, cold anger echoing through the beautiful, austere room, 'Is that the important question you want answered? Why should you ask that? I thought you knew! You told me so, didn't you—in more than polite language too Wasn't "promiscuous" and other such terms used?'

Those lids fell, and ruthlessness wiped away all other expressions. Dominic spoke, and although anger didn't show through as it had in her speech, the girl drew in her breath at the tone his words carried when he answered her.

'I want a straight answer to my question, Letitia, that's all! I asked you what went on between you and Madison that night?'

Anger again took over from the apprehension which those ice-cold words had generated. 'What business is it of yours? For heaven's sake, Dominic, let's finish this. That dreadful night has been dismissed from my life. It was just unlucky we ever met. So now let's both go

91

about our own lives as if we'd never done so. Please . . .
please, Dominic, take me home.'

'Yes . . . afterwards. Just tell me about you and
Madison first.'

She turned away and moved towards the door.

'It's locked,' said that inimical voice.

'Then you'd better unlock it,' she answered.

'Yes . . . afterwards!' he said again. 'I've told you
what I want!'

Letitia stood stubbornly silent. If he thought she was
going to discuss in detail what had happened that
night, either before or after he came upon the scene, he
had another think coming!

'Look, Letitia! I've been told something of it, but I
want to know absolutely. I swear if you don't answer
me . . . just one answer to one question . . . we're going
to have a replay of the last half of that night—in there.'
He pointed to the hallway where a half-open door into a
bedroom was just discernible.

'Oh . . .' her lip curled, 'so now we come to the
reason for this abduction! I wouldn't havé thought you
needed to employ such methods to get girls up here.
However . . .' Her shoulders shrugged as her acid
words stopped.

This time she backed more sharply as Dominic
moved purposely towards her. Her foot caught against
the leg of one of the small tables, and she staggered. An
arm went round her—an arm, hard but impersonal.

'So what's it to be, Letitia? In there,' he gestured
towards the bedroom door, 'or one truthful answer?'

It wasn't going to be an easy answer. Letitia said,
gazing blankly across his shoulder, 'I don't understand
you. It won't make any difference—the damage is
done! But as I want the affair to be finished, and as
undoubtedly you've heard something tonight . . .'

'I made it my business to speak to young Madison . . .
about why he wasn't dancing. I wondered why he
wasn't with you—both at the farm and tonight at the

dinner and dance.'

'Oh, well . . .' she gave a long sigh and thought she had better get it over with, so continued, 'Peter came out to help Johnny when it seemed there was trouble among the tobacco.' Her voice sounded even, expressionless. 'He fell into a roll of barbed wire—rusty barbed wire, which Johnny had left in the way. He was slashed and hooked. I helped clean him up and sent him to my doctor for a tetanus shot and to have it dressed properly.'

The saga finished as far as she was concerned, she stood silent in a room that held an atmosphere she couldn't define.

Then Dominic spoke, and his clipped harsh tones held a cutting edge. 'You couldn't have told me that when I came into your house, I suppose?'

'Did you give me a chance to? You began to tell me what . . . what you considered me, right away. I couldn't understand what you were saying. I thought you were drunk!'

'It would only have taken a few short words to stop . . . ' This time it was Dominic who abruptly halted, apparently memory overtaking him.

'Yes, well . . . when I became really frightened—on the bed,' the words came out now, stifled, strained, 'I did begin to tell you, and you leaned over me . . . and . . . and . . .'

Two brown hands were outflung. Dominic said, 'I know. I suppose there's nothing I can say or do . . .'

But tiredly, Letitia turned away and stood staring at the shut door, her back to him.

'I suppose too,' and, strangely, Dominic's tone had changed back to his normal one of cool pleasantness, although if she had been looking at him, she would have seen the strain showing, and that for once the deep emerald eyes were wide open, 'I suppose too,' he repeated, 'you wouldn't stay and have a cup of tea with me? I didn't feel like eating at the dinner tonight.'

It was with incredulity that she swung back to look at him, the unexpectedness of the outrageous suggestion bringing back awareness of ordinary things . . . of everyday ordinary things.

She couldn't move; she couldn't believe what he was saying. And suddenly she looked directly at him, shaking her head in disbelief.

'I really am hungry, Letitia,' he went on. 'And I really couldn't eat at the dinner tonight. Now you, I expect, ate everything that was set before you, conscience clear—the only thing on your mind besides enjoying yourself was keeping as far away from my vicinity as you could. Oh yes, I did see that,' he continued, as her head came up. 'I also saw, even if I didn't know what I do now, the way you behaved. It wasn't what one would expect, believing what I did about you.

'So . . . you do remember, don't you, that you once invited me to have a cup of tea with you—and I accepted. You *could* reciprocate that gesture.'

Letitia couldn't get more outright disbelief into her expression at what he was suggesting. For him to compare the two events was just inconceivable!

He said, 'I promise you I won't bring up any subject you wouldn't like. I promise you I won't touch you . . . It's really only a cup of tea.'

She gazed at the closed door, then looked helplessly again into that dark handsome face—friendly, impersonal, eyes wide open, not, as they usually were, hooded. However, any expression they might be holding was so far back it was indecipherable.

Letitia shrugged, and as if he had taken that gesture for acceptance, Dominic turned quickly, and reaching another half-open door, switched on the light.

As she came forward, he drew back from the doorway, and she walked into the kitchen with yards of space between them. It was another such gleaming modern room as the one in his Mareeba home, only this one was in pale jade, not golden yellow.

Letitia glanced down at the tiles her shoes had echoed on as she moved from the deeply carpeted lounge, and a wintry smile tugged at the corners of her mouth. Her shoes matched the inlaid tiles exactly!

Dominic was over by a bench filling a kettle. Letitia walked over to the big windows. This room didn't look out over the ocean as that great expanse of glass in the lounge probably did. She found herself gazing instead over the city. There were still lights ablaze—but not as many as earlier on. It was getting late.

'Get the cups, Letitia, will you?' asked that friendly voice. So, turning from the lighted street, she glanced about the kitchen, then moved across to glass-enclosed cupboards set high above a bench separating the small breakfast nook from the kitchen proper.

They held china, so she reached up to bring forward the large breakfast cups, bypassing the afternoon-tea crockery. Anyone could drink tea, she thought, on any occasion, but food . . . She didn't believe for one moment that Dominic was hungry. So why . . .? And then she decided she knew why.

Dominic was going to make the North his home now, and he really wouldn't want the rememberance of what he had done surfacing every time he saw her. His insistence now on this little event was to clear the way to a casual, nodding acquaintance which would be remarkable to no one.

'Letitia . . .' Startled out of her thoughts, she glanced up quickly. Dominic was gazing across at her, and those emerald eyes of his were glinting. Now what was up?

'Will you eat Italian bread, Letitia? It's very crusty, but tastes wonderful.'

She looked at him, and said gravely, 'Yes, thank you. That would be nice.' What else could she say, remembering the words she had hurled at him on that certain night?

'But to make up for that,' Dominic was continuing, 'we'll spread it with Australian ham, and then, I think, some good English mustard. Now how about that?'

Letitia couldn't help it—she gave a small gurgle of laughter, and Dominic turned away to begin slicing bread. She didn't see the tiny smile of satisfaction which came to curl those sculptured lips.

When, a minute or so later, he put two plates on the table, one of them before her, she eyed it with a tinge of misgiving and said, 'May I have a knife, please? I couldn't get my mouth around that!'

'For shame, Letitia! What about the hundreds of hamburgers you must have eaten in your young life?'

'I don't eat hamburgers.'

A dark eyebrow went high, and hurriedly she went on, 'But I do eat fish and chips. They're my favourite food, eaten out of the paper—with plenty of salt and vinegar.'

This time it was the man who gave, not a gurgle, but a shout of laughter. He said, when he had finally stopped, 'Right, next time we eat, that's what we'll go and buy.' He began to stir sugar into his tea and, between eating, remarked casually, 'I hope the rain lets up, not only because of this farm visit tomorrow, but because I don't think they want it up at Port Douglas either.'

'Port Douglas?' Puzzlement echoed in Letitia's words.

'Yes, it's a beautiful place, Port Douglas. And our company is building that big tourist complex up there. That's where I was the last fortnight . . .' Dominic broke off. Oh, of course, she thought unhappily, that was where he had been when, on returning, he had walked down to their farm on being informed about the trouble in the tobacco.

'Letitia!' Startled by the tone in which he had said her name, she came out of her abstraction to glance up swiftly. His hand had reached across the table, palm up. She looked at it. Dominic saw the intention in her expression, but before she could push back her chair to rise and leave, he spoke quickly, laughingly. 'That Peter! He certainly put his hurt leg to good use today. A wounded hero home from the wars couldn't have played on it as much.'

'Yes,' she took hold of this innocuous subject right away, 'yes, I noticed, and was so thankful. Look, Dominic, it's late. I'd like to go.'

'Anything you say, Miss Forrest. But at least you ate my sandwich.'

Letitia actually smiled directly at him, and said, 'Yes, I did, didn't I? And I expect it's only fair to tell you it was delicious. Thank you, Mr Catalano.'

'My pleasure! OK, let's go.'

But as she went to stack the crockery, he said sharply, 'Leave it!'

And with only two words there was suddenly a new dimension colouring the whole atmosphere. To both of them, those words conjured up another time they had stood together in yet another kitchen. And abruptly, everything he had done to her was gone with the wind. Space was there between, a table was a barrier. Yet there was no distance between them as far as Letitia was concerned. She was back in those arms, conscious of only magical caresses that played havoc with every nerve and sense she possessed. And, memory surging, she shivered. . .

Coming to her was the recollection of a heavy body spreadeagled right across her, and with laughter deep in his throat, a voice that was saying, 'You will respond, you know!'

Together they gazed across the few yards separating them . . . and it was Letitia's hand this time that went out entreatingly towards Dominic as she said his name.

But he had turned sharply away, and glancing down, she saw a hand gripping the table edge, the normally long brown fingers showing white with tension.

'Stop it, Letitia!' he said. And then in a different tone of voice, he went on, 'You know, I thought I knew myself—until one night I found myself capable of rape. But at least on that occasion, emotionally, I maybe thought I had a reason. But tonight! I knew what I was doing, what I was going to let myself in for, and still felt confident I could give a promise—and keep it. But I find now I can't even keep my word . . .'

'Dominic . . .' Breathless, hurrying, the one word was all she could get out. Then she said as she had said once before, 'It doesn't matter, Dominic . . . it doesn't matter!'

He turned right round to look at her then, and, shocked, she saw reflected in the wide-open vividness a look of intense dislike—directed at her! She couldn't believe it! She gasped. Why . . .? They stood for a long moment, a moment seemingly of eternity to the girl as they looked at one another, the room silent about them.

'Yes, well, one learns new things every day,' said a cool, crisp voice. 'Come along, I'll take you home.' It was incredible, politeness was the only expression visible in both manner and tone.

Dominic walked towards the door—not passing her, but going the long way round. And by the time Letitia had made herself follow, he had unlocked the front door. He stood holding it, his gaze downbent.

She said again, and it again echoed breathlessly, 'Dominic . . .'

All he did was open the door a little wider, so, helplessly, Letitia went before him. She heard the door slam shut, and felt this alien Dominic step softly behind her. At the car, also politely, he opened the door.

Outside, the rain had degenerated into a mere

drizzle. Letitia sat in her corner, watching the wipers play back and forth across the expanse of glass.

'What's the number of your unit, Letitia?' he asked. And she thought unhappily that Dominic had spoken her name for politeness' sake only, as if she were someone he barely knew.

She told him, and outside it, with the other units around theirs in darkness, he held out his hand, saying, 'Give me your key.'

She dropped it into the fingers held cupped for it and stood there quietly—what else could she say or do after seeing that look?—while he unlocked the door. He reached in, switched on the light, glanced around, then handed back the key. He waited until she had stepped inside, reached out a hand to swing shut the door, and she was left staring at the place, empty now of his presence.

It wasn't my fault, her mind was saying. I didn't do anything! But she *had* done something. Abruptly, and inexplicably, all her anger, her frightened dislike of him had vanished, and she had known that she would have stayed there with him, been to him whatever he wanted—if he had reached out one beckoning finger.

Oh, well, tomorrow was another day. And she would have to learn to live with it.

CHAPTER NINE

THERE, that was the last curtain pegged out. Letitia walked away from the line of flapping washing and settled down in the long armchair. She gazed up through the tracery of leaves and decided that the sky above today wasn't a clear lapis-lazuli. The high arch was a deep indigo. It was the end of June, and winter up here did mean coolness, but it also meant blue and golden days with seldom any rain.

She thought defiantly, I'm all right now! I am!

This coming weekend was a month away from the Cairns farm outing. And she knew that for the first couple of weeks after it, she hadn't been all right.

Flopping into the back seat of the Kellys' car, she had settled back as Les eased the vehicle into the stream of cars heading for home after the morning's visit to, of all places, a mango plantation. Letitia hadn't felt much like gathering information, though.

But once out of the heavy traffic, Les turned his head and said, 'You know, we're only in tobacco, but this weekend has been an eye-opener. Don't you think so, Marge?'

'Yes, I expect it has,' answered his wife. 'But I think we'll stick to tobacco, Les. We're doing all right at it.'

'OK then, if you think so, dear.' Les didn't care. Easy-going, he was as happy to farm tobacco as any other crop.

Letitia lay back, closing her eyes. It was very easy to feign tiredness, because it seemed as if every bone, every muscle in her body, had to be forced to do their job. But there had been one plus, Dominic had not been there!

When finally arriving home, she had discovered she was caught up in a lethargy that stayed with her. She couldn't sleep; she found she couldn't eat. But as the days passed, she worked among her mango trees. She spring-cleaned. She stayed up late to watch television. She read—but she didn't read any sort of romantic novels.

She stayed away from the town, coaxing Johnny to do the shopping. She heard from him that Dominic was away, and then that he was back. Then one night, late, she had been reading a thriller, and an unexpected passage had her in Dominic's arms. The book fell to the floor and, turning her face into the pillow, she felt the tears sliding ever more rapidly down her cheeks. She cried for a long time—for lost dreams that would never come true now.

But the next morning, dressing, she knew she would definitely have to make plans for a new life. Then, brushing her hair before beginning to tie it back with a piece of old ribbon, she halted abruptly, and looked closer.

Horrified, she searched her face. Ebony shadows showed under eyes that appeared haunted. She knew she had lost weight, of course she did, but she hadn't realised until this moment that with her height and figure, she looked almost gaunt.

And her hair! That really made her panic. She had always been proud of its immaculate shining fairness, but now . . . She stood for a second, motionless, shock taking hold. Then catching up the brush, she brushed and brushed, until finally she combed it out and let it lie free on her shoulders. Then, in old jeans and a T-shirt, she went through to the kitchen, her step carrying a firmer, more positive tread.

Fixing Johnny's breakfast, she drank her own orange juice, then deliberately made herself scrambled eggs. If she could eat toast, as she had been doing, she could make herself eat scrambled eggs. And she was going to go into town today. She had that new life to plan.

Her new car would be there on Friday, she was told at the car showrooms. And then, going to his office to pay Peter's tetanus-shot bill, she met the doctor emerging with a patient. He smiled at her and said, 'Hello, Letitia,' before a frown gathered between his eyebrows.

'You can come next,' he told her, and before Carol could say she hadn't an appointment, Letitia found herself thrust before him into the consulting-room.

'What have you been doing to yourself?' he asked, his frown going deeper.

She threw out a placating hand to this man she had known for always. 'I had a little bit of a personal worry,' she explained, 'but it's finished now, I promise you! And, Dr Elder, I've decided I'd better make some plans. What do you think of my trying for university?'

'I think it's a good idea, if you want to. But to study what?'

She smiled at him and saw his doctor's eyes watching her face. She *had* really had a shock this morning, and he would probably see the change too. However, that was all going to change. She said now, 'I don't really know, but there should be something I'm good at, surely?'

'Have you ever thought of nursing?' asked that kindly man who was studying her so closely.

'No, I haven't. I've never given it a thought,' she replied, a slight frown between her eyes. 'I've never had much to do with sick people—except Grandfather, of course, and I loved him.'

'I know. But do you realise, Letitia, that if you did do nursing, and finished your training, the world is your oyster? That piece of paper is a passport to anywhere.'

It was these words that decided her. And the man

across from her smiled in satisfaction as she sat up straighter. Still, for a moment she didn't answer, but then she said, 'That might be just the thing. But how would I go about it? And I'd want to train somewhere else. I wouldn't want to train here at Mareeba.'

She received another keen look, and then Dr Elder was saying, 'Well now, just leave it with me. I have a friend on the staff of the Townsville hospital, I'll see what's offering. I'll be in touch.'

And he had been in touch, so that this afternoon Letitia was going to the hospital to register as a volunteer helper—to help her get some idea, the doctor explained, of hospital life.

After lunch, Johnny escorted her outside, and as she stepped into the little new green Gemini, he bent down to say, 'I think this whole idea is stupid, Sis. If you feel you must do something, why don't you train here? You don't need to go away.'

Gazing into his troubled face, Letitia knew she couldn't say to him—I have to go! He would be demanding instantly why she *had* to go. She couldn't say, either, I want to go. He would have been hurt. So she told him an outright lie.

She said, 'Look, Johnny, there's no opening for me here. And you know I won't be going for months. Anything could happen.'

His face cleared. To this young brother of hers, months away was a lifetime. Yes, anything could happen.

She drove away, still finding the need to watch herself with different gears after years with the big Holden. Through the town and up to the hospital, she found her way to the car park. Outside she leaned back on the shining green enamel to glance about her with a proprietorial look. Living here all her life, she had never actually been inside this large, rambling building.

Oh, well, she had an office to find. But she discovered

that asking for the Matron's had her pointed its way immediately. She did find herself a bit nervous when raising her hand to knock, but on the 'Come in,' she told herself not to be silly.

'Oh, Miss Forrest, Dr Elder tells me you think you might like to help us?'

'Yes, Matron,' she answered, and found the interview was almost over before she knew it. A busy woman, this one! Letitia rose, finding that Thursday was the day she had to come. On her way out, she was halted with her hand on the doorknob.

'Oh, Miss Forrest!'

'Yes, Matron?'

'Wear a comfortable pair of shoes.'

Glancing down at her high-heeled white sandals, Letitia grinned, and found herself saying, 'Yes, I will, Matron.'

Looking back over her shoulder, laughing, she opened the door and went through. Then she gasped— for two reasons. Without looking, she had bumped into a heavy body standing there with its hand raised to knock, and she couldn't believe what she was seeing.

'Letitia!' it exclaimed in astonishment. And then, after a more prolonged look, 'What in the name of heaven have you been doing to yourself?'

She went to move hurriedly past him; but her arm was taken, and in no gentle grip either. She found also that although she might not know her way around this place, Dominic did.

It was a busy corridor; she couldn't pull away and run, so she found herself in a small, empty room with a door closed behind them. She also found herself being thoroughly looked over.

'There's no sign of an accident. Have you been ill?' asked that pleasant, familiar voice.

'For heaven's sake, Dominic! Do I have to meet you everywhere? I'm in a hurry. I've got to go.'

'Yes, all right,' he answered. 'But first . . . you look . . .'

She could hear the echo of the words he had used in his unit in Cairns. Ringing in her ears were 'Yes, afterwards, but first . . .' in almost the same tone.

However, this was a different place, a different time.

She said bleakly, 'I know how I look. But I've told you, I'm in a hurry. I have to go.'

'You were coming out of the Matron's office. She doesn't see patients or people there, usually. Unless . . . are you . . . have you decided to take up nursing?'

Letitia didn't want to answer him. She didn't want him looking her over as he was doing. It brought back too many memories; memories she had learnt, oh, so recently, to keep out of her thoughts. However, she also knew the way his mind worked.

So she said bluntly, 'Yes, I have decided to go in for nursing, but not here . . . never here.'

These last words did make the expression on his face change. It closed up, and the heavy eyelids fell.

'OK then, so what were you doing in that office?'

As she remembered that look of sheer dislike which had been her last remembrance of him, anger found its way out.

'It's simply none of your business, Dominic, where I've been or what I do. Still, for that matter, what were you doing going into that same office?'

'I had a perfectly valid reason. I'm a member of the hospital board, you know . . . Is that a laughing matter?' The last few words were not delivered in his usual pleasant tone, for she had begun to laugh, in long silent gasps.

For suddenly she had found it funny. A member of the board . . . and she having an interview for a job as a lowly volunteer helper! She said, 'No, I don't expect it is,' and added, 'I didn't know, but it's still none of your business what I'm doing,' and she turned to leave.

His tall figure was suddenly between her and the door. 'It *is* my business when you look like that,' he told her.

'OK, then.' She drew in the needed deep breath. She had found that, with Dominic, keeping her own counsel didn't work, so . . . 'OK, then,' she repeated, 'it's a long story, but it probably happens to everybody . . . especially to young girls. I met a man, and being, as I said, young, and . . . inexperienced, I thought myself in love with him. Why shouldn't I have done? He was all that any girl might hope for—tall, good-looking, and, or so I thought, kind and caring.'

She brought her gaze back from his shoulder over which she had been looking, to see with even a little satisfaction that a tinge of red had crept up beneath that tanned, handsome face. She continued regardless.

'The first time he made love to me, it wouldn't have mattered what happened, or what were the consequences.' She shook her head at his suddenly upflung hands, then said, 'It's better to finish it now, Dominic; then you can really pass me by with just that friendly nod you once mentioned.

'However, what happened between us the second time . . .' Here she found she needed extra air, more breath to go on, 'allowed me to get over that infatuation; it allowed me to hate . . . to put him out of my mind.

'If you'd left that situation as it was then, Dominic,' her breathless, hurrying voice continued, 'everything would have been fine. But you didn't . . . you wouldn't. And in your unit in Cairns, after that dinner and dance, I found the hate and dislike I'd erected as a barrier had dissipated, that by being with you again, seeing you act so charmingly, I . . . I . . . But you know how it ended! And I found myself having to come to terms with yet another dismissal. But don't be conceited, because I got over it—completely. It's finished!'

A long brown hand was outflung once again, and Dominic went to speak. Letitia interrupted, 'It is, Dominic—for me, finally finished! And you should be pleased about that, because you probably have all the feminine companions you need. In fact, there's been talk about a very beautiful one you've been seen around with in Cairns. So really . . . just let us be ships that once passed in the night, because when I leave here I don't expect to see you again.'

She *had* been told of the gossip—casually by Johnny, and very interestedly by Marge Kelly, who had come out to see Letitia when she heard she had the virus—the story she had had Johnny put round.

So now she repeated, 'I must go,' and walked to the now unimpeded door. But other words halted her.

'Yes, she *is* a beautiful girl. Her name is Serena Tulio. But I would like to tell you, Letitia,' that pleasant, soft voice, carried now an edge of deep amusement, 'that although she might have been seen—weren't those your words?—around with me, she has never been up to my apartment in Cairns. Nor has any other female—except one!'

Letitia had begun to twist the doorknob, but now she felt her cheeks flood with colour, and angrily she turned. 'I really do hate you,' she told him, looking directly into eyes that were now gleaming emerald pinpoints. 'And all I want from you from now on if you do happen to see me, in the street, or at any other place,' her hand gestured around the room about them, 'is to please just nod, as you once promised to do. And now I *am* going.'

However, Dominic said quickly, 'But you must know you'll be seeing me on Sunday night.'

Her hand on the door-knob, she turned to glance back at him. 'No,' she returned. 'I didn't know any such thing. And I certainly will not be seeing you—on Sunday night or any other night. Why should I be?'

'Don't you answer your telephone?' he asked.

Puzzled, she only looked at him.

'I'm sure Marge Kelly has rung you—or has tried to, either yesterday or last night—about a barbecue out at my place. To raise money for our farm outings.'

'I was out among my mangoes most of yesterday . . .'

Interrupted, Letitia found she was being spoken to curtly, arrogantly, as Dominic said, 'Looking as you do, you had no right to be grubbing about in the paddocks. Haven't you any bloody sense?'

Astonished at the words, at the tone in which they had been spoken, and especially at the language she had never before heard Dominic use, she gazed up at the hard face above her for a long moment, then said, 'I have every right to do exactly as I want to do.' She added maliciously, 'As for last night—Johnny was on the phone for hours, talking to Giovanni. Your manager has been most helpful, you know.'

'He had orders to be,' Dominic had spoken absently, as if not thinking. And suddenly, abruptly, Letitia saw a different man in front of her.

He had been a farmer before—albeit a probably rich and successful one, who lived down the road! Oh, yes, attractive and assured, and of course—oh, yes, with a charisma that surrounded him—she acknowledged that. But now, with those few careless words which had been spoken so absently, she saw him as the successful businessman he was. Used to giving orders, and used to having them obeyed.

Oh, well, that was Johnny's business. She was definitely going to be out of it all—and as quickly as she could manage it.

Again she said over her shoulder, 'I won't be coming to that barbecue. I'll have another date arranged for that evening, when or if I'm contacted. So as far as I'm concerned, it's just as well I *was* out among my mangoes yesterday when the phone was ringing.'

Then, hesitating for a brief second, not wanting to speak as she was going to do, she said, 'Dominic, I really don't want to see you or have anything at all to do with you again. And as I'm leaving the district, I'd like——'for a second time she hesitated, trying to search out the words she wanted, 'I want . . . these last few months sponged right off the threads of my life. Please . . . I'm not coming to your place ever again.'

'You show your youth, Letitia, saying such a thing.' No laughter, no sign of softness, coloured Dominic's voice when he answered her. 'Even in my circumstances, which I'm able to manipulate quite well, I've learnt you can't always do only what you want, or have happen only the things that you plan. At all times I thought I could command my own destiny, but,' two hands were thrust outwards in a throwaway gesture, 'one lives and learns. So, I expect I *will* see you on Sunday night!' His hand went out in a dismissing wave, and it was almost blindly that Letitia walked through the door, along the busy corridor, to emerge into bright, brilliant sunshine.

Finding her way to the car, she sank down on to the seat and tried to see her way through those words of Dominic's. She couldn't understand them. Oh, well, it didn't matter. She was going away soon, and she was going to forget him. She was! And she wasn't going to that rotten barbecue either.

She drove home, not even thinking of the car beneath her being new. And when she arrived, she found she *was* going to the rotten barbecue after all.

Johnny called to her from among the tobacco plants. He came across, saying, a wide grin almost splitting his face, 'Marge Kelly phoned. They're having a barbecue at Dominic's on Sunday night. I told her that yes, of course we'd come. Won't that be fantastic, Sis? Oh,' belatedly he remembered what she had gone into town for, 'did you fix everything up at the hospital?'

And at her nod, before she could say anything else, he had departed at a run, almost as busy a person as the Matron.

Slowly Letitia turned her footsteps towards the back of the house. She realised now that there was no way of not going. It was unfair! She said to herself through clenched teeth, 'OK, Dominic. I've got to come to your barbecue, and much good may it do you to flaunt me as just the girl who lives down the road . . . a neighbour and a farmer you're obliged to ask. I'll be going to Townsville soon, and it will be a long time before I come back!'

CHAPTER TEN

SO ON Sunday evening, Letitia gazed assessingly at the reflection looking back at her from the mirror. Yes, the jeans were barbecue dress, and the scarlet top cut like a man's shirt with a split on either side, was of soft cling-ing wool. It highlighted cheeks that were beginning to get their colour back. The face was still thin, but the dark shadows were only that, and were fading.

She smiled happily at her hair. It was certainly back to normal, and lay turned under like a medieval pageboy's, gilded and shining about her face. 'OK,' she called in answer to another impatient shout from Johnny, 'I'm coming!'

But she still lingered, unwilling to start. She unstop-pered the small perfume bottle and dabbed the glass top to her throat and wrists, then could find nothing more to delay her. Oh, well, she thought, at least I don't look too bad. That's a plus, I suppose.

In five minutes they had arrived, and, taking the needed deep breath, Letitia went forward to greet whatever the evening had in store. And it was there, waiting for her.

'Good evening, Mr and Miss Forrest.' And giving her brother a playful punch and telling him to go find a drink, Dominic was over.

'A very great improvement,' he told her softly. 'Enough to have half the men in the vicinity vying for your attention.'

'Oh, not half of them, surely?' she replied, giving him the most brilliant smile she could dredge up. 'Wouldn't there be one exception? But still, I'll have a look round

111

and see what I can come up with.'

Suddenly she wasn't looking into the friendly face which had greeted her. In the uncertain illumination which hung from trees and posts in this outside barbecue area, those vivid eyes showed no reflected gleam. Hooded, they made his face unreadable. However, before he could answer, Les had walked over. 'Come along, Letitia, I'll buy you a drink—one like Marge's. How about that?'

Dominic laughed and strolled away. Letitia smiled, and allowed Les to pilot her to where his wife was waving. But it was Dominic who had all her covert attention. Dressed as he always was in high-fashion clothes, immaculate in tight fawn trousers and a white cashmere roll-collar sweater, he was as eye-catching as that Roman god of old she had once compared him to. She sighed deeply.

I hope, she thought acidly of the tall departing figure, you get all splashed while you're cooking the steaks!

But she should have known better. She saw as he joined a small group congregated on chairs set away from the brightly lit cooking area that it was Giovanni, in a tall chef's cap and white apron who was wielding a long fork and busy tongs.

Deliberately, glass in hand, Letitia gazed about her, searching for someone she could have beside her to laugh and talk with. She almost jumped out of her skin when a voice said astringently from behind her, 'Well, thank the lord for a familiar face!'

Swinging round, Letitia grinned at Dominic's cousin. 'What are you doing here, Joe?' she asked. 'You're not a farmer.'

'No, I'm not, thank goodness. I have better things to do with my time. And I don't know what's come over Dominic! I've come up here twice lately and fallen into a party. Giving parties is simply not like him at all.'

'Oh, well, enjoy yourself while you may. It could be

later than you think . . . isn't there an old saying
something like that? And there are drinks to drink, and
food to eat, and lovely girls to enjoy yourself with. You
do realise, however, that present company is always
excluded,' Letitia laughed up at him.

Joe laughed back at her, saying, 'We'll see, but for
now don't you go away. Wait until I find Dominic and
let him know I'm here.'

She didn't go away. Joe was just what she needed.
Then he was back, telling her, 'Come along, I've only
got until ten o'clock.'

Wondering why only until ten o'clock, Letitia went
along. Along to where the tantalising aroma of grilling
meat came wafting to them on the evening breeze.
They collected their steaks. And, glancing at her plate
after all the salads had somehow got on to it, Letitia
shook her head.

Then as they strolled towards a big gum tree,
abruptly Joe scuttled away and, amazed, she was left
gazing after his disappearing back.

But he had returned in seconds to spread a rug on the
grass. Glancing at its quality, she raised her eyebrows.
'Are we allowed to go scrounging for things like that?'
she asked, not wanting to borrow anything uninvited
from the owner of this place.

Her hand was caught and she was being pulled
down. But, sitting cross-legged laughing at the face
laughing back at her, Letitia felt a look roving them
both. She knew whose it was, of course she did! And
turning carefully, she saw it passing right across her . . .
and then, just as assessingly, across Joe.

Her teeth clenched, and again she felt the colour hot
beneath her cheeks. Dominic had no business to be
even looking at her, never mind in the way he was
looking. However, she also knew she shouldn't be in
his neighbourhood. How had she been manoeuvred
into coming here?

Then, turning her back on that deliberate, evaluating look, feeling it as a physical shining line that stretched between them, she made herself speak. She said to her companion.

'Sorry, Joe, what were you saying?'

'I was asking you, Letitia, if you'd ever seen a game of football'

'No, I haven't,' she answered, only absently, still feeling the force of that glance upon her. 'Except perhaps,' she continued, 'the boys playing against another school in the school grounds.'

'You should come down to Cairns and watch a match,' Joe said.

'I don't think so,' she still spoke absently.

'Look, come and see me play next Sunday.'

'Don't be silly!' answered Letitia—and then, suddenly, gave her attention more completely to her companion. 'Oh, sorry, Joe,' she said contritely, 'I really didn't mean to speak like that. It's just that I don't know anything about football.'

'Then it's about time you learnt. Everyone knows about football.' Her companion was most emphatic.

These words did catch her out of herself and made her laugh. 'Oh no, not everyone, Joe. I've never ever seen football being played.'

'It's about time you did, then. I'll come and pick you up next Sunday.'

'Don't be silly,' she said again. Then she glanced up swiftly as a presence loomed over them. Joe looked up too. 'Hi, Dominic,' he greeted his cousin. 'I've just been telling Letitia I'll take her down to Cairns to watch me play football.'

'And what are you going to take her in?' came the caustic reply. Letitia looked at him quickly. She was beginning to recognise all the nuances in Dominic's voice by now, and this one sent a shiver through her.

'Why, my car, of course,' Joe was openly grinning.

'If she wants my advice, she'll stick to a sport she already knows, and avoid football and speed maniacs who use that dangerous mountain road as a racing track,' said that inimical voice.

And where before she had had no intention of accepting, Letitia now said contrarily, 'I think I'd like that, Joe. Thank you.' And defiantly she looked up into those wide open vividly green eyes before the lids fell, hiding any expression. But tension and static was an invisible force enclosing them both. Then Dominic turned to stroll away to his other guests.

And suddenly the food was uneatable again, and Letitia pushed the half-eaten dinner aside. Not so with her companion. He went on busily chewing. He also grinned, as one young man, on his way to the busy cooking area, scuffed a toe on the rug beneath them and said, 'Unfair! I can't sneak inside and snaffle one of these to spread carefully in a dark and lonely spot.'

'What gives you the idea,' answered Joe, 'that I needed to sneak inside and get hold of it there? I'll have you know I came here in my car, and I have that vehicle prepared for any eventuality.' He joined cheerfully in the crow of delighted laughter that greeted his words and went calmly on to finish his meal.

But a few minutes later, after a glance at his watch, he rose and reached down a hand. 'Come along,' he told her. 'I'm off to get some of Rosa's dessert. I'm not missing that!'

He certainly didn't miss that. He was given a piled-up plate, but Letitia, refusing, said quickly, 'Can I have a glass of wine instead, please?'

Joe handed it to her and she put it to her lips. She knew she didn't particularly want it, but the clear shining liquid was cold and welcome to her tongue. At least she had something to hold in her hand like everyone else.

Another presence came to join them, another wrist

was raised to be looked at. 'It's almost ten, Joe,' said the familiar voice of Dominic. 'If you don't get away and pick up your mother at the hospital, you'll have her coming all the way out here to look for you.'

'Heaven forbid!' Hurriedly, Joe put the last of a pastry into his mouth, and with it half full, spoke through it. 'I'll have enough listening to all the details of Aunt Angela's illness on the way home—you know how Mother is about family. It's not fair, Dominic. You keep yourself safe in this fortress of yours up here, and in that other fortress you have in Cairns, where you can't even be got at on the phone because you have an answering service. And *that* always says you'll be rung back, which is a lie, because I've yet to receive a return call. It really is unfair,' said Joe for the second time, 'that while both of us have aunts and uncles and cousins coming out of our ears, I'm the one caught up in their affairs, but you never seem to be there to be bothered.'

'It's after ten,' was all the tall man beside them answered.

'Oh, all right! Letitia, I'll ring you. I'd better be off.' He was off, and Letitia was left standing to watch two departing backs this time—one dark, the other fair.

She swung round sharply as someone said loudly, 'Oh, really, wouldn't that just happen for Dominic!' And gazing beyond the speaker, Letitia saw, lifting above the horizon, a huge full moon. It seemed to drift upwards in seconds flat, and, serenely rising in its orbit, was gilding the tree branches with silver while etching their shadows in ebony blackness.

Then, as if on cue for a film in the making, the music started. It wasn't the rock-'n'-roll stuff she had heard and jived to, in that house behind her the last time she was here, in Dominic's arms.

It was what Johnny called smoochy music, and it was doing its job, because couples, gaily and with laughter, were already dancing on the smooth grass to its call.

Dominic must have switched it on after seeing Joe off.

With the rising of the moon, a cool breeze seemed to have sprung up, and feeling suddenly quite cold, Letitia went to stand beside a fire now beginning to die down. Placing her wineglass on a bench, she smiled, noting that it was empty without her even knowing it, and went to hug arms about herself while thinking that it was stupid to feel cold. She *did* have on a wool shirt, if not much underneath it. She gazed around for her brother, wondering if he would be ready to leave. He was one of the dancing couples.

'Put this on,' said Dominic's voice from behind her. He was holding out a sheepskin coat, which by the size of it must belong to him. She shook her head.

'Look,' he was placing it about her shoulders, holding out one sleeve for an arm to be slid through, 'it's about time you took more care of yourself. You might need the least possible clothes up here in summer, but night-times in winter can be cold. This is the second time I've seen you almost shivering. For goodness' sake, can't you be a little more sensible?' The words came from above her head, hard, harsh.

Obeying the sound of them rather than the words, she slid her arms into the coat, and found Dominic's fingers closing it about her. Then, abruptly, she was drawn on to the lawn and into his arms.

It was too much, she thought confusedly—the delicate, insidious music closing around them as they turned slowly to its beat, the beauty of a night flooded with silver, and Dominic . . . Oh yes, Dominic.

She felt his heartbeats thudding against her breast like far-off hoofbeats galloping over heavy dessert sand, and suddenly she didn't care. She didn't care about what had happened, what was going to happen. She twisted her body into the hard length of the one holding her, and gave herself up to whatever the night would bring. Because this was Dominic, after all, and he was the only man she would ever love. Under her breath she spoke his name.

She found herself swung out around trees, then behind a large trellis which blocked out all sound of a party enjoying itself. Dominic's hands were beneath the enveloping coat. He didn't speak. He just pulled her into the confines of his own body, and, curves melting into hollows created to receive them, they stood, fused together . . .

'Oh, Letitia, I want you!' muttered an unrecognisable voice, and lips that came down to move slowly and gently across her own sent reason and the mundane world flying to the wind. She wasn't thinking . . . the people, the party . . . everything had gone. There were only kisses, caresses, sending the static of electricity coursing through her. It sent her standing on tiptoe to clasp her arms tightly about his neck; it sent her pliant body to arch even more completely into the one holding her so fiercely.

A hand suddenly spreadeagled low upon her back brought her more closely into him, and she gasped. Then the other hand was undoing the buttons of her scarlet shirt, and Dominic's lips were roving up, down, and across, and Letitia knew she had passed into another world.

She wanted to say—take me away, Dominic. Don't end it . . . as her head fell backwards over the arm holding her, while his lips and those long fingers played their own different kind of magic, over smooth naked skin.

Dominic's head rose a little, and he looked down at her imprisoned in his clasp. Looked down at the entire body exposed to any action, any desire he so wished; at the cascade of gilded hair silvered by the moonlight as it lay dishevelled across his dark, tanned arm. But most of all it was at the closed eyes, lashes making half-moons across cheeks flushed a deep rose-pink, and at lips which were even now murmuring his name.

He stood, every tense muscle of his body hard against her. He stood, with his every heartbeat pulsing his need as he held her to him. Then he spoke, oh, so softly, deep in his throat—and she couldn't understand it. The words were uttered in Italian.

Then in English, as he moved away a little, 'This is no good, Letitia. Look, it has to be straightened out. I'll see you when we're both in our right minds.'

Her hand went out to him in a fluttering movement . . . she couldn't believe it. She shook her head, saying, 'You can't . . .'

But he could. 'You don't have to tell me,' he said harshly, 'who's to blame for this little episode. I know I am! I think I know what I'm doing. I tell myself I have everything under control. However, I find that with you it's a different matter altogether.

'And I've got a yard full of guests out there. I do have to leave you! I don't want to, but I must.' His form slid from out of their ebony patch of shadow, into bright moonlight, and then he was gone.

Leaning against the trellis at her back, Letitia made an attempt to bring her breathing back to normal, to . . . she reached into her jeans pocket for her compact. Moving more into a patch of brighter light, holding the small mirror at an angle that allowed her to see, she gasped, then muttered, 'Oh, no! I can't go back looking like this!'

Glancing at her, the least discerning person would notice the flushed cheeks, the blazing crimson of lips which owed nothing to artificial colouring just now, the bright hair falling every which way.

Deliberately, coldly now, she ran the tiny powder-puff over and across her face, until her cheeks had lost their burning deep-rose impression. She lipsticked her mouth until it was scarlet to match her shirt—but a lip-sticked scarlet, not the bright vividness that those scorching, branding kisses had imparted to its curves. Her hair didn't need much attention, merely a few swift strokes of the small comb.

Then, she was positive now, if only she watched her eyes, she could retrace her steps with impunity. But abruptly she remembered . . . and with still shaking fingers, she fastened up the buttons of the red shirt.

Then, about to shove her hands casually into her pockets, she found with a wry grin that she had to hitch up the coat a little. This she did, and, easing round the trellis she gave a thankful sigh. God, or fate, or whatever, was looking after her. A group of youths were congregated where she could easily stroll up to them. She did.

Johnny saw her. He said, 'Hi there, Letitia,' then with a glance around and observing a much more sparsely populated area, said, 'Time to go home?'

'I think so,' she nodded around the small group, knowing them all, and as the brother and sister walked away, Johnny grinned. 'Never be the last to leave, wasn't that what we were taught, Sis?'

If she had felt like it, Letitia would have laughed. As it was, she said, 'Too right!' and stiffened when her brother said, 'We'll go and say goodnight to Dominic. There he is over there.' And of course, because she had to, she went.

He was chatting with three older men. Nearing them, she began to ease off the coat. He couldn't possibly see her, she thought acidly, but he said, 'Leave it,' and she thought she would never hear those two words without remembering Dominic.

But their host was turning and speaking in that pleasant, easy voice he could use. He said, 'Letitia felt a little cold, and Rosa found a coat for her. We really don't want a relapse of that virus she had, do we?'

'Actually,' said kind old Mr Fenton, 'I thought she looked a bit under the weather last time I saw her in town. Feeling all right now, my dear?' he asked.

'I expect my mangoes think I am. They've been getting a thorough house-cleaning.' She smiled her most brilliant smile at him, and received what she wanted, laughter from them all . . . no more mention at all about any virus. She added, 'Thank you, Dominic, for a lovely party,' then smiled and, turning, departed with Johnny.

At home, she hung the sheepskin coat on the outside of her wardrobe—and left it there. She was finished with trying not to think of its owner, as she had attempted to do after the first aborted love scene, and that dreadful second one . . . and the almost third one in Dominic's unit in Cairns.

From now on she was going to think of him as much as she liked—always recognising, however, that nothing would come of the relationship. But she was going away soon, to begin nursing, and she had been assured on good authority that she would think of no one or nothing but her aching feet, for quite some time.

By then Dominic and his image would have receded, deliberately pushed far back in her memory. And if sometimes, at a particular scene or memory, it jumped out to hit at her—oh, well, that was how life was.

So now, purposefully, she walked into the bathroom to wash her face, to cream it leisurely. She was not ever again going to allow people to think she 'looked a bit under the weather'. She was going to make herself look as lovely as she could be made before going to Townsville. Strong, and glowing with health. She *was*, she decided fiercely.

And if, she reflected, as she went back into her bedroom, switched out the light and climbed into bed, she filled in the waiting time with thoughts of Dominic, only she herself would know . . . Remembering, among so many other things, how his heartbeats had thudded against her, how his almost unrecognisable voice had said, Letitia, I want you!

And it would only be herself who would know how much she had wished he had exclaimed, Letitia, I love you!

But I don't care, she thought, as she had done twice already tonight. And gazing out into the brilliant silvery night, allowing her reflections to travel a mile or so down the road, she muttered softly, 'What are you doing now, Dominic? Not thinking of me as I am of you, I bet. And though you said you were to blame, I was too . . . just as much!'

She wondered about his conduct. After the dance in Cairns, he had seemed to want to set things right. He had tried; he had been so nice, until . . . Restlessly, she turned.

Was he committed to something or someone? That Italian girl, Serena—she was everything any man could want. Beautiful, and from the same sort of people from which Dominic came. But he had said, with that wicked pirate's gleam in his eyes, 'She hasn't been up to my apartment, though, Letitia.'

And then, inevitably, thinking of him, she was back in Dominic's arms, body fused to his body. But she found she was not being caressed by scorching, demanding kisses; she was being cradled in arms that held her seductively close, as they danced dreamily and slowly, to that smoochy music of Johnny's.

Her eyes closed; the brilliant night outside was drawing now into another day, and she was still in those arms when she fell over the borderland of deep unmoving sleep.

CHAPTER ELEVEN

UNEXPECTEDLY the next morning, as Letitia was preparing Johnny's breakfast, the telephone rang. Carelessly, wondering who could be calling at this early hour, she walked across to pick up the receiver.

'Hello, Letitia speaking,' she said into it.

'Yes, Letitia,' came the last voice she had expected to hear. And for a moment she couldn't concentrate, shock causing her to stand silent, rigid with disbelief. But Dominic was continuing, 'I did mean to come to see you this morning, but I have to go up to Port Douglas. In fact, I should be on my way already. There's been a spot of bother on the development site—and as millions of dollars are involved, I'm afraid I have to go up and see if I can do some trouble-shooting.'

Receiving no reply, he said, 'Letitia?'

'Yes,' she answered again with just the one word. She didn't know what else to reply to that urgent, hurrying voice.

'Are you all right? You don't sound all right!' Abruptly, the tone of the voice had changed, taking on a more personal note.

Quickly she said, 'Yes, I'm fine' And as a different sort of silence came over the wire to her, she added, 'I truly am all right, Dominic!'

'OK. Look, I could be away one day, or all week, but I should be home at the weekend. And, Letitia . . .'

'Yes?' she said again, as he paused.

'Our acquaintanceship hasn't been all clear sailing, has it? And for that I admit I'm mostly to blame, so I intend to rectify it at the first opportunity. But for now, I

123

didn't want to leave here without some sort of communication . . . to have you think all kind of things—especially after last night.'

Another pause echoed across the line, this time a longer one, then Dominic was adding curtly, 'I'm not going to apologise for any of my actions! That would mean I'm sorry they occurred, and I'm not! Right, then, I'll see you when I get back. So long!'

Before he could replace the receiver, Letitia broke in breathlessly, 'Yes, so long, Dominic. Take care.'

Low, but coloured with amusement, the reply came, 'Oh, indeed I will! Going down that hazardous range in the hurry I'm in, flying to Port Douglas in that two-by-four plane . . . and then taking the risk of getting a worker's hammer over my head—oh, indeed I'll take care. But thank you just the same for those two kind words, Letitia.' The line went dead.

Replacing her own receiver as if laying it down on extra-sensitive eggshells, Letitia stood motionless. It showed, this call, that, even being in the hurry he was, Dominic had thought of her, and possibly of the chagrin she might feel if he had just gone away, especially after that scene . . . the one he was not sorry for. As for herself, it sent her pulses fluttering to even remember that torrid episode of passion and desire acted out behind a flower-laden barrier.

And she wasn't sorry for it, either. So as she had decided, until she went away she would think her own thoughts, dream her own dreams.

The week went by with Dominic's presence remarkable only by its absence. And yesterday, Saturday, while Letitia was out attending a kitchen tea for one of her school friends, Johnny had told her the phone had rung for minutes, but by the time he had got to the house it had stopped.

Letitia took this news calmly. It could have been anyone! It could have been Dominic! But the phone had remained annoyingly silent from then on. And now she had almost finished dressing to go to Cairns for the football.

Having no idea at all what one wore to that sport, she had donned jeans, and a hip-length blouse which she had tied in a knot at her waist. And she had added, a trifle wryly, a cardigan to her canvas carryall. She wasn't going to be caught getting cold this day. Tonight didn't matter; Joe had promised faithfully to bring her straight home from the game.

So with a last satisfied glance at herself, she walked through to where Johnny was waiting by the car—the new car. He was going to Dimbulah to some 'do' up there with Mario.

'Drive carefully,' she said, and grinned.

'I will,' he answered. Then returning her grin with a wider one, he added, 'And you see that Joe does the same.'

'I will,' she replied, and watched them drive away.

They passed Joe coming along the driveway. At least Letitia thought it must be Joe. But he was certainly in no vehicle that could by any means be used, even by a driving maniac, to race down that dangerous range road, whatever his cousin had intimated.

'Hi there,' he greeted her, stepping out and taking her bag. 'That's what I like—females to be punctual.'

In the car and out on the main road, she smiled around at her driver, saying, 'What a lovely little car you have. I'm so pleased! But by the way Dominic spoke, I thought you'd land up here in a Porsche, or at the very least, an Aston-Martin.'

Joe returned her smile. However, there was a furrow between his eyes. 'It's a damned funny thing,' he said. 'I've got a Jaguar . . . not one like Dominic's. Mine's an E-type. We all own Jaguars of some kind—the company gets a discount. But mine went suddenly on the blink, between last night and this morning too. If I didn't know better, I'd think it had been got at! I simply couldn't understand it, or find out what was wrong—and neither could Dad, who knows his way around every kind of engine. I wanted to borrow his big Jaguar, but he said he needed it himself, so with all the reluctance in the world I had to settle for this. Believe me, I'm not happy about it.'

'Oh, but I am.' Sending a wide, radiant smile his way, Letitia settled down to enjoy the day. Her driver couldn't be a racing maniac in this little car.

It was a pleasant drive before they got on to the range road, and it was turning out to be a happy outing. Actually, she had never been out like this before, for a whole day with just one person—even with Peter.

Still, she wondered why this cousin of Dominic's had suggested this expedition. Why come all the way up here for her? He was pleasant and friendly; he had made not the least sign of a pass at her. Oh, well, she thought, shrugging, the world turned on its axis; time brought what time brought. She would enjoy the day as a nice ordinary outing. It would be a change from the emotional stress which had coloured some episodes of her life lately.

'Do you like seafood, Letitia?' Joe broke into the small silence that had fallen in the car, and jolted from her thoughts, Letitia smiled happily at him.

'I love seafood,' she answered. 'In fact I like almost all foods. Why?'

'There's a restaurant specialising in seafood on the esplanade. I thought we might go there for a fairly quick lunch.'

'Anything you say,' she acquiesced.

'Is that so? Well, actually, I had intended taking you home for the meal, but as you know, my parents had to go up to Port Douglas. I don't expect you'd like to come there just the same? I cook a mean chicken and almond Chinese.'

Disappointment spread through her. What a shame! She hadn't wanted this pleasant day spoilt. Suddenly, inside her, an acid smile formed. Wouldn't it be just lovely if inadvertently Dominic walked into a scene like one that had already occurred, and this time with his cousin . . .

She answered this modern equivalent to, 'How about coming up to see my etchings?' lightly. She said, 'Do you know, Joe, I've just remembered that although I told you I liked most foods, I find I really don't care for Chinese chicken and almonds.'

The figure behind the wheel doubled up with laughter. Just as his unmentionable cousin did! she thought wrathfully. She exclaimed aloud, 'Look out! You'd better watch the traffic.'

'I'm watching the traffic. I really couldn't be involved in an accident in this apology for a car, Letitia.'

'That's what every young man says,' she answered more than a little tartly. 'And what did I say that caused all that uncouth laughter? I thought it was a perfectly normal remark.' Again she spoke acidly.

'Yes . . . yes, it was. But if you think back you'll remember that I said—I don't expect you'd like it. I expected you wouldn't. But, sweetie, you can't blame a bloke for trying. It's a pastime in this day and age.'

'Yes, I know, but . . .' She came to a stop, not knowing how to put into words her own attitude.

Suddenly Joe was laughing again, but in the ordinary, normal way. He said, 'I really am quite happy with the way things are. And that I have a charming young guest to eat my restaurant lunch with, and who later on will watch me win. Take that troubled frown off your face, Letitia, because look, here we are!'

They were swinging through the city now, and gazing out, Letitia noticed the boutique where she had bought her lovely tangerine dress, of which Dominic had said as he went to fetch the car, 'Stay here, you don't want to get your beautiful dress wet.' Oh, heavens, would everything she saw and heard remind her of him?

She nearly asked her companion then if he knew where his cousin was, but stopped herself in time.

Joe pulled into a slot on the esplanade, and they sauntered through a warm golden day, among the casual Sunday morning strollers. Then with a glance at his watch, Joe asked, 'You won't mind if we eat early, will you, Letitia? It's twelve o'clock now, and I have to be at the grounds by two.'

So they went inside to what was an almost empty restaurant with just one or two tables occupied.

Joe handed over the big menu when it arrived, but, smiling across at him, she said, 'As I told you, I love all seafood, so you order for me, Joe—but not a big meal.'

'OK, here we go,' replied her companion. 'I don't want a large meal either—I'm playing soon. And,' he smiled across at her, 'as I'll have someone charming and lovely watching me play, I'd better see about winning!'

They ate small pink shrimps in a tart, luscious sauce, then a dish of crab meat, dressed only with hot melted butter. Neither ordered dessert as they sat over their coffee, idly talking.

'Have you always lived here?' she asked him at one point.

'Yes, always. Born here, went to school here, and most likely, I'll go to that big wild world in they sky from here.'

Smiling at his words, Letitia said, 'You sound as if you like the place.'

'I do. I wouldn't want to live anywhere else. What about you? Do you like Mareeba?'

'Do you realise, Joe,' she answered him wonderingly, 'I've just never thought about it . . . but it's only now occurred to me that it's the one place I want to live in also, except . . . I won't be! I'm going away in a few months to train as a nurse.'

Her gaze roving the dancing, scintillating blue waves of the ocean before her, she didn't see the quick glance Joe cast her way, or the faint frown that overcast his face as he looked consideringly at her. Then it was gone and he said, 'I don't want to hurry you, but I think we'd better be off.'

They parked among what seemed thousands of cars, and then Letitia was piloted into the grounds and up rows of steps to a seat in a grandstand.

There he said, 'Now don't move from here when the game is over—I'll come and collect you. I can't have you wandering around like an innocent abroad among a football finals crowd, I'd never find you. You understand me?' He had turned and run down the stairs.

So she sat in her reserved seat, wedged in by bodies on either side, and understood then Joe's admonition about staying where she was until he came for her. In this vast crowd she could very easily get lost.

She also found while looking at the game that you could understand its purpose. One lot wanted the ball to go one way; a different lot wanted it to go the other. She also realised suddenly that she didn't know what team Joe played for, or what colours he would be wearing.

So when the big match started she asked a man beside her, 'Could you tell me, please, which team a man called Joe Peterson is playing in?'

A finger pointed. Then as the time passed, she began to understand about crowds going wild at football matches, and she didn't like it. She sat on the edge of her seat just praying for it to end.

The man beside her suddenly leant down and told her, 'I think it's your friend who's just been hurt.'

Startled, Letitia saw a stretcher being carried off the field. Pushing past rows of legs, she hurried to the players' exit.

'What happened?' she asked Joe. 'Are you badly hurt?'

'It could be a broken leg,' said the man standing beside them. 'He's to go to hospital.'

'I'm sorry, Letitia,' said Joe. 'Wouldn't you know this would just happen today! Look, you must ring Dominic—I'll give you his number.'

'Yes, later,' she answered, having no intention at all of doing so. 'But for now I'm coming to the hospital with you.' She did . . . in an ambulance.

The next few hours passed in a kaleidoscopic sound of crisp voices, quick movements, and the antiseptic smell of a big outpatients' department. Finally she was admitted to see Joe, plastered and bandaged. He told her, 'Letitia, here's Dominic's number. Get on to him, and he'll take charge of everything. He'll have to let my parents know. He'll have to take you home . . . if only he's there at home himself. But he must be. He's not up at Port Douglas, or at his own home at Mareeba, because I rang there when I found unexpectedly that I had no car.'

Unconsciously she began to shake her head, but Joe interrupted. 'I'm sick, Letitia. I don't want the worry of you on my mind. Dominic will see to everything!'

So, because she had no option, she went to the phone in the corridor. She told the voice that answered her who she was, about Joe, and where they both were, as concisely as she could manage, then she went back to Joe.

'Did you get through?' he asked, and at her nod, 'But not to Dominic personally, I'll bet,' he added wryly.

'You'd be betting right. No, I got the answering service,' she told him.

'If only he checks in, everything will be all right then. Dominic can fix anything.'

'For heaven's sake, stop worrying, Joe! I'll be fine. I'll

stay here until the visiting bell rings, then I'm off. But first, do you want to know what I think of your football game?' And she told him!

Hearing a loud burst of laughter, a nurse put her head round the door. 'Really, you should know better,' she spoke sharply to Letitia. 'And you, my man, had better settle back.' She tidied up an already immaculate bed, and almost flounced out.

Joe was abruptly shaking with laughter, albeit an almost silent one, with an eye out for intruders. 'I really don't believe you can say such things, Letitia,' he told her softly, and began laughing all over again.

Then, as a bell rang, his expression lost all merriment. He said, 'Get my wallet from that drawer, just in case Dominic doesn't come, and you have to go to a motel.'

It was Letitia's turn to laugh now. 'Really, Joe!' she exclaimed. 'I've been on tennis tournaments since before I left school, and anything can happen at them . . . I always carry money, and a bank card. Don't be silly!'

Unexpectedly, she saw him relax on the pillows, all anxiety wiped from his expression. Good, she thought, then saw that he was looking over her shoulder. She swung round.

A man was standing in the open doorway. For a fraction of a second she didn't realise who it was. Then of course she did! Although he wore an unfamiliar business suit of dark navy, the pristine white shirt with its hard collar caused that handsome dark face to stand out. And she saw also that those eyes, colour indistinguishable with the distance between them, showed as only two glinting pinpoints.

He walked into the room. He did glance at her as he passed. He said, 'And what in the name of sport have you been doing to yourself?'

All he got back was a wide, complacent smile. 'It's not what I've been doing to myself, Dominic, it's what those blokes I played against have done to me! I don't really think, however, that they had any need to break my leg.'

While they were speaking, standing so close to him, Letitia thought, He's different somehow. And it wasn't only the unfamiliar suit, either, that was puzzling her. She noticed that a lock of hair from a usually smooth head had fallen over his forehead. That also, in catching the light, it showed a tinge of lightness in what she had always thought was dark hair.

Even his demeanour was different. Gone was any sign of anger, of arrogant demand . . . or the ruthlessness he so often showed in her presence. And then she noticed the voice that was so much a part of him. The cool, concise crispness was absent. It carried now, in speaking to Joe, a soft slur.

Startled from her thoughts, she glanced up swiftly as Joe said to her, 'Dominic will see to everything, Letitia . . . he'll . . .' He broke off as a nurse entered the room— a stiffly-starched staff nurse, from her epaulettes.

She was beginning to say, 'The bell has gone; you'll have to leave . . .' when Dominic turned round. He looked at her, at all of her, and Letitia could see it happening.

He told her in the soft silkiness of this new voice, 'Nurse, I'm Dominic Catalano. I have an unlisted phone number, so would you give this to them at the office, and say to get in touch with me immediately if my cousin's condition changes? Do you think you can do that for me?'

It's just not fair! reflected Letitia. Of course he could have that little thing done for him. He could have anything he asked for done for him.

He smiled at the pretty nurse, was smiled back at, and then had taken Letitia's arm, though only loosely, guiding her from the room. And suddenly she saw what was the other something that was so different about him. He had been drinking! Something she had never seen before.

He walked her down the corridor, pushed the elevator button, and inside, stood away from her. She smiled at him, suddenly friendly to this different Dominic. She said, still smiling, 'You *have* been enjoying yourself!'

This did make him look directly at her. He saw that smile, and said, in his new voice, 'And with everything else, you add tolerance to your virtues! But no, I have not been enjoying myself. I've been stuck over a lunch which I hardly ate—and all the rest of the day with two businessmen from the south, two bank managers, a lawyer . . . and a tough old buzzard from Port Douglas who owns too much land, and who thinks he can drive a hard bargain.

'However, I think . . .' a low laugh escaped the figure leaning against the far side of the lift, 'I only think, mind you, that our company has what it wants! And I might also inform you, Miss Letitia Forrest, that all the others are in a worse condition than I am. I am *not* drunk, Letitia, although I may be a quarter on the way to it. But again I can inform you that I know exactly what I'm doing.'

Letitia laughed at this easy, different Dominic. 'I'm sure everything you say is true, Dominic. But look, here we are,' she interrupted herself as the lift stopped, then asked him, 'So now, with all that expertise and ability which Joe is so sure you have, can you find me a taxi?'

'Of course—that's the easy one. I have one outside waiting.'

'A taxi waiting? How could you have?'

'Come along and see.'

She went—and saw. Dominic opened the back door to usher her inside. 'Give him the name of that motel the Kellys and I stayed at, Dominic. I'm known there,' Letitia instructed, before sinking down on to the seat.

The driver was spoken to, and in the back, her companion sat in his corner as far from her as he could get. He didn't speak, so she found nothing to say either.

Busy with her thoughts, Letitia was surprised when the taxi pulled to a stop. She had thought it would have taken longer. And then, gazing past Dominic who had opened the door, she saw the sheen of water, and with a quick glance to her other side, a big dark pile that was a large apartment building.

'Dominic . . .' she began.

'Come along, Letitia,' said that new slurred, soft voice.

'No, look, Dominic—just tell the driver I'd like to go to that motel.'

'Yes, afterwards.'

Letitia knew that in the years to come, wherever she was, whatever happened to her life, those two words would always bring Dominic to mind.

He was paying the driver now, who said, 'Thanks very much, but what happens now?' as he looked over his shoulder at his still stationary passenger.

Dominic said, 'Letitia!' and his voice held not the slightest sign of a slur now. She descended from the vehicle.

Watching it drive away, she unconsciously hugged her arms around herself. A cold breeze was coming sharply off the ocean. Then, remembering, she began to reach into her big bag for the cardigan she had added to its interior. She made herself stop. Not again, she thought. I'm just simply not going to allow him to see that I'm cold.

But this time her arm was taken, and she found herself walking up steps, with a tall, silent figure behind her.

Inside the unit, there was no need to flip switches. The whole place was ablaze with light. They faced one another in its brilliance.

'If you think for one tiny little moment that I would allow you to go to a strange motel alone at this time of night, you really have another think coming, Letitia!' And abruptly, so suddenly, that slur had quite disappeared from Dominic's voice. It was back to the familiar bleak, ice-cold tone she had heard him use to her on other occasions when he was angry.

However, she made herself say reasonably, 'Half-past eight, Dominic—that's not late.'

'As far as you're concerned, it's much too late to go booking into a motel on your own.' He glanced at his watch. 'I also suspect,' he was adding, 'that it's too late to go out to dinner. And speaking of dinner, I vowed that before another of these situations happened between us, a lot of things would have to be straightened out. But it appears that besides our getting off on the wrong foot from the very first, it seems to be happening to us all the time.

'I tell you, Letitia, I simply never envisaged us having supper up here again together, until . . . Still, I can't take you home to Mareeba. I simply wouldn't dare drive that range road tonight after the day I've had, and especially not with you in the car.

'So, I need food, and lots of coffee. But first a shower. Now . . .' he threw out a hand towards the hallway, 'please be my guest.'

CHAPTER TWELVE

HAVING no option, Letitia walked before him. He opened a door into what must be a guest-room. 'Five-star motel accommodation, no less, instead of the three-star one I intended going to!' she said ironically, as she gazed at pale ash furniture set on deep-piled green carpet, heavy Thai silk curtaining the windows in cream folds.

'It's not motel accommodation—in fact, we'll have to make up the bed. I have leave to inform you that with a different attitude I'd never have the place to myself. I have uncles and aunts and cousins galore, as you've already once been told. So the word is out! I don't have a spare bedroom,' said Dominic from just behind her.

'Oh, yes, I think I do remember an occasion where you told me you had cousins . . . female cousins, I think, were mentioned. And that they were looked after properly, not like . . .'

She broke off. The face that was opposite to her now had changed dramatically as Dominic cut in, 'Don't push your luck, Letitia. Especially not tonight! Tonight, I might not have the control I always pride myself on having. I do remember that occasion—and I also remember telling you on the phone that I apologise for nothing—and that night is included. In fact, I remember . . . some of it with distinct pleasure.'

Letitia felt a rush of hot colour stain her cheeks. And as their glances met and held, that familiar flash of tension was again between them, holding their two motionless figures in a field of electricity. Her breath caught.

And gazing into those vividly green eyes, wide open this time, she felt the room, the space around her, disintegrate. One moment longer and she would have collapsed into him. But Dominic had stepped sharply back. He said, and his voice held strain, harshness, 'Can you find sheets to fit that bed, if I show you a linen press? I'm afraid I wouldn't make a success of that.'

'Yes, I expect so. Where's the cupboard?' Letitia knew she was speaking, and she knew what she was saying, but it simply didn't register. Only that electrifying tension of a moment ago was vivid and real. Then she was walking behind him as he went down the short hallway.

She reached up to take down green sheets from among orderly piles, adding pillow slips. Dominic's tanned brown hands collected towels of the same colour. Back down the corridor, suddenly Letitia caught her lower lip between her teeth to prevent laughter bubbling out.

Here they were, for all the world like a host with an unexpected guest—which she was—going through the mundane housekeeping chores of making up beds. Dominic Catalano! She felt the almost hysterical laughter well up again.

His glance, passing over her as he went to drop his bundle on to the bedside chair, came to an abrupt halt. 'And what the devil,' he asked sharply, 'are you laughing about?'

'I was only thinking . . .' and suddenly she was laughing out loud. 'Sorry, Dominic, I just realise that from what you said about uninvited guests not being your scene, here I am, unwanted, uninvited . . .'

'All too true. This would have been the last idea I'd have dreamed up. And really, Letitia,' his voice had turned grim, serious, 'it's not the best thing that could have happened. Behaviour has occurred between us even when I knew—or thought I knew—exactly how I would act. But tonight . . . tonight's a different kettle of fish. So, if you'll excuse me, I'm going to shower.'

'Very well.' Letitia went to turn away, then halted as Dominic spoke across his shoulder.

'This is one time I do apologise to you, Letitia—leaving you like this instead of seeing to a meal at once. Still, can you amuse yourself, or even——' suddenly gravity disappeared, and a wicked, glinting smile gazed back at her, which, added to that unfamiliar fallen lock of dark hair on his forehead, made him an altogether different person. He repeated, 'Or you could even take a shower yourself. You've had a long day as well.'

He was gone, closing the door behind him. Letitia turned, leaning her back against it, gazing at the room about her. Oh well, she decided, when in Rome, do as the Romans do. I *will* have a shower, but first I'll make the bed. Pulling back the thick quilted cover, the same colour and material of which the curtains were made, she tucked in the bottom sheet, then folded the top one back over it.

There were no blankets visible, and she certainly wasn't going to go searching for any. She would have to wear the same clothes again, she was thinking, looking through her bag to see what she could find. But only make-up, wallet, a book, and a knitted headband she sometimes wore on the tennis court met her searching fingers. And of course, she thought wryly, the cardigan, deliberately added in case she needed it.

On her way to the bathroom she was stopped in her tracks. There was a knock on the door. It was repeated as she made no answer—this time accompanied by her name.

Making herself move towards it, wondering, because hadn't he said so definitely that he was leaving her? she opened it. She looked up into his face—and suddenly her stomach turned over. She had never seen Dominic like this before—dishevelled, half undressed, shirt opened and over his trousers, as if he had taken it off and then replaced it; with hair ruffled and disordered even more than it had been.

His gaze met hers, saw the expression it held, and slid away. 'I've brought these for you, Letitia, just in case you might want them. You needn't worry that they . . . they're new and haven't been worn.' A bundle was dropped into her hands, and once again she was gazing after a disappearing back. Moving backwards, she kicked the door shut, and over by the bed saw what her hands were holding.

Her fingers spread out pyjamas made of heavy maroon silk. She left them lying there and marched to the bathroom.

Turning on the shower, she stripped, then felt laughter start to bubble up again. This was certainly not a prepared motel suite, and she completely accepted Dominic's statement that it had never been used. There was no soap!

She used more than her share of water, allowing it to sluice over and over her then, with a towel wrapped sarong fashion about her, she went back into the bedroom. Of course she was going to wear the pyjamas. Her other clothes had been on all day—however, she shook them out and hung them neatly over a chair-back, before turning hesitantly to those folds of heavy silk outspread on the bottom of the bed.

Slipping into the top, she went to stand before the mirror. Why had she been so reluctant about wearing it? Actually, it could have been a long mini. It reached almost to her knees, and with the heavy silk falling

fully about her, showed not the slightest contour of
her figure, even without a bra which she had left off.

Once, twice, three times, she folded back the cuffs
of the sleeves, finding it hard to accomplish as the silk
slid about so. Now she saw she definitely couldn't
wear the bottoms. The waistband came almost up to
her neck, and the legs flopped on the floor over her
feet. She discarded them.

She went across to the window, gazing out over the
same view she had looked upon from the kitchen,
remembering that last time she had been here, when
Dominic had prepared that funny little supper with
Italian bread, Australian ham, and English mustard.

Oh, yes, she remembered; she remembered everything about every encounter she had had with
Dominic. But for now, she had better not think of
hands that had made her heart jump as they caressed
bare sensitive skin, or scorching kisses . . . She
backed away from the window, and with her hair
combed, lips lipsticked, she walked outside in her
maroon silk and bare feet. Lights blazed everywhere,
so she left her own on and the door open.

She glanced round the familiar kitchen, but had no
intention of touching anything . . . then she saw the
papers. Today's! Taking up the national Australian,
she settled down on a chair to read. She had got
through most of the headline stories when, without
hearing anything, she knew she was not alone.

Dominic was standing in the doorway, and
suddenly everything was back to normal again.
Dressed in grey slacks and a grey roll-collar pullover,
he looked as if he had wanted to tone down
everything—and his hair showed the same usually
dark smoothness, with no falling, random lock that
gave to his face a devil-may-care look.

'Coffee first, I think,' he said, coming right into the
room, and busied himself with a percolator. 'Could

you face bacon and eggs, Letitia? he called over a shoulder, and she answered, 'Yes, please.'

At that reply, he turned and smiled at her. 'OK,' he answered, 'here we go.' But suddenly he swung back. 'I don't often miss much, but this evening was exceptional. However, while I was in the shower I did wonder why you didn't ring your brother to come and get you.'

'Because he's up at Dimbulah with Mario at some big Italian affair . . . and so are Rosa and Giovanni. I didn't even think to ask the host's name. I knew Johnny would be all right with the others. However, I was going——' she hesitated for a moment before continuing, 'I was going to ring Giovanni's number when I got to the motel, and leave a message.' She wasn't looking at Dominic; she was watching the coffee drip into the glass container.

But she *was* surprised when he left the kitchen, without even answering. She heard him on the phone, then he was back. 'That's fixed,' he said. 'I got on to Giovanni himself. He'll give Johnny the message.'

Letitia wondered what that message had been. But her shoulders went up in a shrug. As Joe had so emphatically said, Dominic would fix everything.

Bacon went under a slow griller. Eggs were being broken into a bowl. Unable to prevent herself, she exclaimed, 'No one's going to eat all those!'

The smile she got back was easy, friendly. 'Oh yes, they are. I need food.' Dominic was beating the eggs slowly with a whisk, and as the meaning of the words penetrated, Letitia's gaze went searchingly over him. His face did show a tiredness, a strain, that was there if you looked for it. He had poured coffee and was drinking it, she noticed, black and hot.

She said suddenly, wanting to help him, 'Is there anything I can do, Dominic?'

And again, over a shoulder, he smiled at her before

answering. 'You could get the china and set the table if you like.' So, laying aside the papers, she found cups they had used before and small plates to match them. She reached up for the larger dinner plates, and turning with them in her hands, found Dominic looking across at her.

'You ought to start a new fashion, Letitia. That sort of dress would go with a bang. And I'll tell you this—you look far too fetching for the circumstances.'

For a change, she didn't colour at his words. She grinned back, a gamine grin. She said, 'I think I look all right too. But I've never felt silk like this before. It gives me such a degenerate feeling, as if I were participating in some Roman orgy.'

'I wouldn't know about Roman orgies. I've never participated in one. As for those,' he flicked a finger at her top covering, 'I've never worn or felt them. They were given to me, two pairs of them, by a business acquaintance in Hong Kong. The ones you're wearing, and a green set.'

Before she could stop herself, she exclaimed, 'I suppose he thought the green pair would match your eyes.' She could have hit herself, because those same eyes were suddenly hooded, but then, thank goodness, almost immediately they were wide open again.

'And what do you think that colour you're wearing matches . . . my dark skin?'

She laughed. Everything was all right again, as Dominic added astringently, 'I'm also afraid bacon and eggs don't fit in with a Roman orgy. And I do think that's a subject I want to keep off.'

Again his words didn't discompose her. What did she care? It was Dominic himself who had to do what he thought he had to do. She was going to go wherever the night took her. He was refilling his coffee-cup.

He had also made tea, which he set down beside her plate. Then he asked, 'Do I say come and get it?' as he slid the scrambled eggs alongside the bacon rashers and set the plates on opposite sides of the table.

'Really, Dominic!' Letitia protested.

'Eat it, all of it,' was the only answer she got.

So they ate their second supper in this kitchen. Dominic spoke about ordinary topics, and she knew she answered him, but, asked later, she would have been unable to describe any of them. Her plate empty, she poured herself a second cup of tea, and with both elbows on the table, slowly drank it.

Dominic didn't waste time. He stood up, collecting crockery, running it under the tap before stacking it into the dishwasher. He turned then and glanced at her across the table.

'Look, Letitia,' he said, speaking slowly, 'we do need to talk to straighten things out. But tonight is not the time, and this place is certainly not the place. We've both had a tiring day, and also . . . I know there's television, and I really could be a more attentive host, but would you humour me and go to bed?'

Letitia didn't answer. What could she say? Then, seeing that tiredness showing so openly now, she flipped a hand, and as she walked past, gave him that radiant smile she didn't often use. She went straight to her room.

But there, feeling restless, she wandered over to the window. As Dominic had said, she had had a long day, and thinking of Joe, a fairly upsetting one, but it was still only around ten o'clock. Oh, well—she moved to the bed and flipped on the bed-lamp, walking to the door to switch out the ceiling light.

She froze. Once again there was a knock on her door. Dominic wouldn't come to her. He had said so, so definitely. He knocked again and called her name.

He said as she opened the door, 'I've just realised we hadn't taken blankets. And as this is the tropics, you know, the air-conditioner is set only for coolness, not heat. I wouldn't have come, except that I have reason to know how cold you get.' He was speaking hurriedly, quickly, not looking at her.

He must have undressed before he thought of it; he was wearing only a white towelling robe. And he was pushing the folded green blankets towards her, wanting to be rid of them. She put out her hands, but was not looking. She only said, 'Dominic!'

And his entire expression changed. 'Don't, Letitia!' Only the two words answered her.

The blankets had fallen to the floor between them, her nerveless hands taking no heed of them as their eyes met and held.

'I didn't want to come back here . . .' the voice sounded so different from the way she remembered it, 'but you do get cold, and you've already been ill. So what was I to do?'

But she only stood immobile, waiting. And then suddenly, as if they were acting on their own account, his hands were on her shoulders, pulling her to him. His lips were on her own, moving gently, softly searching. She collapsed into him, going to where she belonged.

Dominic pulled them apart. He looked down at her, then said, 'You understand . . . you know what will happen! I wanted it differently, but I want you so, Letitia!' His arms went round her and she was swept up, while with those silent, stalking strides of his, he had moved down the corridor and into his own room.

His arms loosened and she slid to the floor, down against the length of his body. Then his lips on hers were a remembered caress, travelling from the corner of her mouth, across her jawline, over the exposed throat . . . she remembered them from another bedroom.

Dominic's head lifted and he said in that strange voice, 'I intended coming out to your place. I intended to discuss our affairs sensibly in broad daylight. I simply didn't expect to be caught into a situation like this. So do you think, *carissima*,' the words came softly to her from against her throat where his lips were resting, 'that some things are meant to be? Because we're going to let tomorrow take care of itself, and see what the gods have in store for us this night.'

Gazing up at him in the big half-dark room, with only a bed-lamp angled towards the ceiling to provide illumination, in a room she wasn't even aware of as passion and desire leaped and played about her, Letitia smiled.

She said, 'I don't know what's meant to be, Dominic; but I've thought my thoughts and made my decisions, and whatever this night brings, I won't be sorry. I promise you!'

Dominic suddenly moved, and his hard tensile body was abruptly stretched against her, length for length, an arm going low upon her back, bringing her completely to him. He told her, and the words were slurred as they had been only a short while ago—but caused by a very different reason.

'OK then, here we go! But first——' His hand was raised and looking at him from so short a distance, Letitia saw surfacing that piratical, wicked gleam which was so familiar. 'But first,' he was repeating, 'I don't believe I need to use force on this covering.'

So instead of ripping a fragile lace housecoat, he busied himself unfastening the buttons of the heavy silk pyjama top. The long tanned fingers went to work, first on one button, then the next, but as they came to the last one her hand went out involuntarily to close over the dark fingers.

'No!' he ordered in that soft, slurred voice. 'Didn't I tell you on another occasion that it was too late to turn back? This time I mean it.'

So she stood with eyes closed as the last button was unfastened, the heavy silk flung wide. And as her eyes opened and she took in Dominic's expression, she felt the heat of colour wash over her, over all of her.

Dominic forestalled the words she was about to utter. He said, and so unexpectedly his low voice sounded amused, 'I did say something tonight, at some place, in another time, about knowing exactly what I'm doing, didn't I, Letitia? But what I said then and what I'm going to do now is, I'm afraid, all outside my control.'

His head came down and she was being kissed, caressed . . . Letitia knew she had been swung up into his arms, and somewhere beyond even thinking, her mind in space, Letitia heard him say, 'Ssh . . .' while a hand went trailing over sensitive nerve-ends. The gentleness he had been using was abruptly gone, his kisses finding a new direction, scorching, desire-laden. She knew he whispered something to her, but she didn't hear it. Her body fused to his, her pulses jumping, she allowed herself to be taken to wherever he willed, to whatever he wished!

She didn't hear it at first. She did know, however, that although Dominic was still holding her, the entire atmosphere about them had changed; she wasn't being kissed, she wasn't being caressed . . .

The phone went on shrilling and shrilling.

'I've got to answer it,' said Dominic's slurred voice. 'It's an unlisted number and only my family has it . . . and the hospital now!'

He reached to pick up the receiver. Abruptly, the

shrilling noise ended, and only the ragged breathing of the man who had slid her down to stand beside him distrubed the air-waves of the large, silent room.

Letitia heard him speak, then tried to free her hand which had been caught between them, and felt the convulsive shudder that rippled through the bare brown skin lying so close to her. She quickly jerked it loose and held it away from his body.

He put out the hand not holding the phone to take hold of it as he said, 'Everything's fine, Aunt Jean. The hospital was to ring me if there's the slightest change. No, you must be mistaken!' Then after a pause, sharply, 'Don't be foolish. Of course you can't . . . Yes, yes . . . oh, very well. Yes, in about two hours.'

The phone went down with a bang.

Dominic had turned. He let go of the hand he was holding, and laughed suddenly, low in his throat. 'What's that old cliché, Letitia? Isn't it something about being "saved by the bell"?'

'I didn't want to be saved,' she protested unhappily.

The tall form beside her was suddenly shaking with the silent laughter that sometimes overcame him. 'Do you actually think I did?' he said. 'But I'm afraid the time for our own affairs has gone. That was my aunt Jean. That stupid clot of a Ben heard about Joe, and instead of going home like a good boy, took himself to the hospital. I have to get up to Port Douglas and bring Aunt Jean back.'

'Isn't your uncle with her up there?'

'Oh yes, he's up there with her. But he's out deep-sea fishing. He's away from all the fuss and bother. *He* can't be got in touch with.'

'I suppose . . .' Letitia asked hesitantly, 'I suppose you have to go?'

'Oh indeed, I do have to go! If it was me in a hospital bed, aunt Jean would drive from Melbourne for me. Oh yes, I do have to go. Because if I even thought of not doing so, I know she'd start out in my uncle Lars' big Jaguar, which she can't drive.

'Now, how do I say goodnight to you, my partner in that wonderfully amorous time just past?' He bent over and kissed her, slowly and lingeringly.

It took him half a minute to dress, to place keys, wallet, and the things a man carries, into his pockets. Then, hesitating a moment, he walked to a wardrobe. Returning, he put a key on the night table. He said, 'I don't want you to leave here until I come back, Letitia. Do you hear me?' And at her nod, he added,

'That's for the front door, which as you already know only opens with a key. It's just in case . . . You won't need it. Oh, and speaking of leaving,' he glanced smilingly across at her, 'didn't I hear you tell my cousin that you had money—and a bank card? Well, it seems very likely that you'll be using one or the other tomorrow, because you're not going home in the morning. We're going to spend the day like civilised people for a change. We'll be going out to dinner properly, also like civilised people. We'll have the proper arrangements made, and time to be ourselves. Understand me?'

Oh, yes, she would understand anything when it was said to her in that tone of voice by the man saying it. She nodded happily. She also grasped the folds of the pyjama top together. She moved towards the doorway to go to her own room.

'Oh, no, you don't!' One strong arm went beneath her, the other pulled down the bedclothes, and deposited her within them, Dominic pulled sheet and blanket up over her. 'If I have to go on this cursed trip, I deserve to have a few nice thoughts to think about. And thinking of you tucked up in my bed will serve very well. Look, I really have to go.' He reached down and ran the backs of his fingers along her cheek. 'Sleep tight,' he said.

And as he walked towards the door, Letitia called after him, 'I love you, Dominic!'

'I know!' was all he answered, not turning round.

She didn't hear his footsteps go down the corridor. She did see the reflection of the lounge light as it went on, and she heard the front door close with a sharp little click.

Giving a big sigh, she reached up a hand to switch out the angled lamp, then settled down in Dominic's bed. Burying her head in the pillow, she lay gazing out towards the faint light outlining the windows. She thought of Dominic—of course. And she remembered, of course, the hour just past. She realised she had brought the whole torrid love-scene on herself. But, and she knew this too, it was only with Dominic that she would have behaved in such a way.

She had had passes made to her even at school. This was today's world, and she was now twenty. She had mixed with the tennis crowd, with the young farmers . . . and she wasn't unattractive. But she had never felt the least need to indulge in heavy petting scenes. With Dominic, however, it was different. She had discovered he was the reason for her whole existence.

She burrowed further into the pillows, and listened to see if she could hear waves washing in from the ocean, then smiled at her fancifulness.

Lying there, drowsily thinking of the day just past—and its aftermath—she knew she didn't want to go to sleep. But her lashes fell over her eyes, and without knowing it she dropped fathoms deep into oblivion.

And it was without her knowledge, too, that quite some hours later the front door was quietly opened, the blazing lounge light switched off, and a soft panther's tread came down the hallway. It passed the

guest-room door without a glance at the still lighted
space beyond.

Dominic stood quietly at his own bedroom door,
listening. Then, apparently satisfied, he undressed
swiftly and walked to the bed. Carefully, silently, he
lifted the bedclothes, and just as carefully eased
himself between the sheets. He waited, and as there
was no movement from the supine figure, he moved
a fraction to turn sideways.

Then, with a satisfied smile curling his lips, he
lowered himself on to the pillows. It was only some
time later, dredged up maybe by a subconscious
knowledge, that the sleeping girl moved restlessly, a
hand fluttering out and a soft 'Dominic' echoing
round the dimly seen room.

He didn't answer, but the satisfied smile grew
wider. And then, abruptly, Letitia was awake,
endeavouring to orientate herself. Her hand touched
the form beside her. She said, now very much
louder, 'Dominic?'

'And who else would you expect to be here in this
bed?' came the drowsy answer. And at not receiving
a reply, Dominic said, 'Go back to sleep, Letitia,
because I tell you, you have no need to even think
about anything . . . anything at all! I'm simply too
tired to do more than just lie here.' Amusement was
the only emotion that cool pleasant voice carried.

'Did everything go all right?' Letitia felt she had to
ask, trying not to be too conscious of the man and his
tone.

'Of course everything went all right. Joe is resting
comfortably in his clean hospital bed. My aunt,
having satisfied herself of this, causing I don't know
how much commotion in the process, is safe in her
own home, and also in bed, I hope.

And of course, that's where I am too. I was
thinking of watching the sun come up with you, but

I'm afraid . . .' A yawn completed the sentence, and, not moving her body, but carefully looking sideways, Letitia saw that those strange, magnetic eyes were shut. Fully and completely closed, this time in the natural attitude of repose.

Dominic was asleep!

CHAPTER THIRTEEN

BUT Letitia wasn't.

And she had no intention of sleeping either, of wasting these precious minutes in unconsciousness. So she lay quietly and wondered suddenly what time it was. She had her watch on, but it was invisible in the dark.

Her glance roving the windows, she noticed unexpectedly that the space around them seemed lighter. Daybreak here in winter would be some time around six, she guessed hazily. But it was certainly not daybreak yet. Probably this was just the false dawn.

Still, little by little, even if very gradually as she lay watching, the space grew lighter until it merged into pale grey. Then, abruptly, she found she could see. And before her glance, the room was taking on an outline; this room she had not even noticed last night, occupied as she had been within a different dimension entirely.

It was a large room, running parallel with the big lounge, she guessed, and having the same windows overlooking the esplanade and ocean. There, was that a flash of light?

As carefully as Dominic had done earlier, only in reverse, Letitia eased herself from beneath the bedclothes and away from his sleeping form, then slipped over the side of the bed.

At the window she saw that it was indeed the break of day, but not yet sunrise. And that there was a window open. She shivered as a cold breeze from across the water struck at her bed-warmed figure.

She looked about her, then picked up the bed quilt which Dominic must have thrown carelessly aside and, wrapping it around herself, sat curled on the window seat.

She sat gazing out over the ocean, and suddenly, without any warning, orange and scarlet was staining the whole horizon. Then in a second, in two seconds, a ball of crimson was emerging from over the edge of the world. Incredibly vivid, it was soul-stirring in its beauty for the brief moments of its coming; then suddenly it was just a vast, mundane golden orb. The sun had risen.

Letitia stayed there on the window-seat for a long while, casting a glance now and then at the immobile figure in the bed which gave no sign of movement at all.

He still didn't stir, even when the street below showed signs of coming to life. Cars began cruising past, children came riding bicycles on their way to school. People strolled their dogs on the esplanade, with the blue of the water beyond, glinting and gleaming as far as she could see. And over it all the just risen sun cast its benign golden warmth.

Glancing at her watch, she saw it was going on for eight o'clock, so again moving quietly, she rose, and dropping the quilt to the floor, stole silently past the bed. On the way to the door she halted abruptly and moving into the bathroom, purloined a big cake of white soap, smiling to herself as she did so.

In her own room, she first switched off the still burning lamp. Then, showering, she lathered herself luxuriously with the stolen soap. She pulled on jeans over bikini pants, and gazing into the mirror, wondered again whether to wear her shirt hip-length or . . . She tied it round her waist.

Then remaking the bed, leaving the sheets on, she glanced round the tidy room. There was nothing she could do about the bathroom, so, picking up her canvas bag, she walked out to the kitchen.

Orange juice from the fridge, which she stood sipping at the window gazing out over a different scene—busy, hurrying crowds on their way to work. But finally, still hearing no sound from the far end of the unit, she filled the kettle, made tea and toast, then sat eating her breakfast, for all the world as if she were in her own home.

What else could she do? She knew deep down in her mind that she wouldn't dare leave without seeing Dominic. And she had no intention of waking that sleeping figure. Again she knew he would wake when he knew he had to.

Finishing her meal, she rinsed the dishes, leaving them on the draining board. Then, out in the lounge, she settled down on the sofa with her book. But it was no use. She didn't turn even one page.

So she lay back, just allowing time to slide over her. There was nothing she could plan for. If she left here today when Dominic woke up, she had her life mapped out; if she didn't . . . It was in the lap of the gods.

And then, sending shock-waves through the austere silent room, came a knocking on the front door. Not a gentle knock, but a very loud and determined-to-be-heard kind of knock.

Letitia sat up straight, her eyes enormous as she gazed apprehensively at the solid door. Then involuntarily her glance went to the hallway leading to the bedrooms. Dominic, in his white towelling robe, was standing there, tying the belt. He looked across at her, and smiled. And her heart went out with such a surge of passionate love that she had to bite her lip to prevent herself calling to him.

A finger on his mouth, indicating silence, he beckoned. She walked across and he said softly, 'Come along,' and drew her into the kitchen.

'Aren't you going to see who it is?' asked Letitia. She knew she personally could not have allowed that incessant knocking to continue.

'Of course I'm not. If it's business, I have a phone. If it's relations, they know better than to come here. And nothing could have happened to Joe in the few short hours since I left him.' Dominic glanced at his watch.

'I don't believe it!' he exclaimed. 'It's way after nine, and I have an important business appointment at eleven. Oh, good.' The last two words were not addressed to Letitia, but apparently to whoever was knocking, as they desisted and went away.

He brought her to lean back against him, and she stood motionless, feeling the hard, tensile length of him behind her. She felt him lift her hair with one hand, the other coming to rest lightly below her breasts.

Then she felt . . . and her eyes closed. His lips were on the nape of her neck, moving gently and sensuously from one side to another.

She thought, Oh, Dominic! and waited for him to turn her round into him. But she was held still.

Hearing the muttered words in Italian, she smiled and said softly, 'I think it's only fair to tell you, Dominic, that I've lived among Italians all my life. You surely don't think I wouldn't have picked up *some* of their language?'

These words did bring action, and she was being turned round to face him. 'Good lord! Of course, I should have expected that. But how much? I wouldn't have wanted you to hear some of the things I've said—they might give you too much of a hold on me!'

Gazing into vividly green eyes only inches away, Letitia would have liked to lie to him, but with Dominic . . . So she shook her head.

'No, I only know some from my schooldays. I should really have taken Italian, but I took French instead. So you're safe for the time being.'

'Thank the lord for that!' Dominic uttered emphatically. Letitia just smiled. She *did* know some Italian.

'OK, then.' He stood her away from him. 'I'll shower, and then we'll have a quick breakfast . . .'

'I've already had mine. Would you like . . .' Letitia hesitated, unwilling to take liberties with Dominic which she would have done with Peter, or, for instance, Joe. 'Would you like me,' she repeated, 'to get your breakfast while you shower?'

For a brief moment there was only silence in the air about them. Then, 'I'd like that very much, Letitia, if you wouldn't mind,' came the formal reply. Then he had turned abruptly away.

So she made his breakfast and, glancing swiftly at him when he returned, attired in an unfamiliar grey business suit, white shirt and a dark grey satin tie, she put it on the table—the same meal he had prepared for them both last night.

Seeing it, Dominic grinned, but he ate all of it mostly in silence. Then, pushing his plate away, he said, 'Now, to business. You're not going home today.' He raised a hand to quell the interruption she was on the point of making. 'No, Letitia, we've never managed to meet in civilised circumstances. To go out just by ourselves, to dine, to dance. We seem to have been always only thrown together unexpectedly.

'So tonight we're going to dinner at the Northern

Heritage, where that kind of leisurely living is on tap. We're going to be served dinner that someone else has cooked—for a change.

'So, I'd like you to go and buy a dress, and the other things that go with it. You'll have to get a complete outfit for our dinner, and you'll most likely need other clothes, as you came prepared for only yesterday. Now,' he added, 'about money . . .'

Letitia's hand went quickly upwards in a negative gesture, but unlike her, Dominic got his interruption in. 'Don't be silly, Letitia. You're here without clothes because of me, so take those notes there and go find yourself a pretty dress . . . one like that tangerine affair you once wore, and whatever other necessities you need.' Across the table from her, the vividly green eyes held an expression that said they wanted no opposition.

However, Letitia answered just as forcefully, 'I don't need your money, Dominic. I have my own—as you probably know, gossip being what it is up home.'

'Very well then,' Dominic's outflung hands accepted her words before he continued. 'The way things are, or are going to be, it's immaterial how things get bought. So just go and get a pretty dress . . . because tonight, come hell or high water, I'm taking you out to the kind of dinner we should have started with.'

'A pretty dress? Really!' she replied acidly mimicking his words. Then, almost disparagingly, she added, 'But Dominic, I should go home. Johnny doesn't know where I am.'

'You can ring telling him you've met an old school friend, or whatever, and are staying overnight.'

'And where,' her reply came even more acidly, 'could I find a school friend to stay with here? I was never sent away to boarding school, I've never lived away. Johnny knows I wouldn't have any friends to stay with overnight.'

'For heaven's sake, Letitia, where's your imagination? Say you've met a young farmer from Cairns and have been invited to a party—unless you'd like to tell the truth and say you're staying here with me. I don't mind!'

They gazed at one another across the breakfast table, Dominic's expression impatient, Letitia's angry.

Then that smile was sent across to her, the one which had overcome any and all inhibitions when she saw him standing in the hallway a short time ago. He wasn't dishevelled and clad in a loose towelling robe, but that smile had the same effect. Of course she would do whatever he asked.

'Very well. Will you fix your phone so that I can ring him, saying I'll be staying overnight?'

'That's my girl!' was all the answer she received as Dominic pushed back his chair.

She followed his retreating back, heard him take his messages, then saw him push the numbers. He was holding the receiver out to her, saying, 'Your home.'

He hadn't even needed to check her number. He had dialled it right away, knowing it. Then Johnny's voice was sounding in her ear. She told him what she had to, heard him answering with delight, pleased that she was going to a party, and finished with, 'OK, love, I'll see you tomorrow.'

'I didn't know before,' Letitia said tartly to the tall man watching with a smile curling his sculptured lips, 'how easy it was to tell lies. I've never done it before.'

'Oh, that was an easy one. But don't ever think you could lie to me.' Deep amusement echoed in Dominic's voice. 'You couldn't! But for now, we'd better be off —I'm very late. However, I'll be home about two, OK?'

He was unlocking the door. He stood back, allowing her to pass, so she went down the now familiar stairs and stepped into the now familiar Jaguar.

Using the back entrance, because she was more familiar with it than the front one, Letitia raised a hand loaded with parcels to glance at her watch. After four-thirty. She hadn't meant to be so late. Still . . . She glanced down complacently at the white and silver box she was carrying.

'Go and buy a pretty dress,' Dominic had said. He had also said when he stopped at the kerb in Abbot Street to let her off, 'Just enjoy yourself today, Letitia. Do your shopping, have some lunch, and I'll see you when you get home.'

Home! But she had only nodded, and went to slide from the car, but his hand on her wrist halted her. 'Take care,' he said. 'I mean, don't go stepping under a bus.'

'No, I won't,' she replied, watching the big car slide away.

So she had gone to a chain store to buy the necessities Dominic had mentioned. She had walked around the big square block that was the main shopping centre of Cairns, until she had arrived where she had always intended going. She had bought make-up, had a milk shake at a pavement café, and had gone to an exclusive salon and had her hair shampooed and blow-dried. Both she and the hairdresser had been pleased with the result.

Now she looked at the solid door, raised a hand carrying the large box with the silver name scrawled upon it, and knocked—knocked more firmly than she normally would. Dominic might be anywhere in the unit.

However, he wasn't anywhere in it. He must have been somewhere close. The door opened almost immediately, and he stood there, smiling at her. His glance took in all the packages and his smile grew broader. His hands came out to take them from her.

'You bought a pretty dress, I see,' he told her, his gaze on the big box. He closed the door.

'I don't know about a pretty one. I've bought a dress.'

'And other things too.' His eyebrow climbed.

'Yes, and other things too,' she replied, returning that look with composure.

'OK, come along in. I've just made tea.'

She didn't believe him, but still she followed. Dominic had just made tea, she saw, and his cup was standing among a mass of papers and print-outs.

He reached down another cup and poured for her, then resumed his seat. 'You won't mind if I get on with this, will you, Letitia? Then I'll have my mind free to enjoy our dinner. I intend to have no outside interference at all.'

Drinking from his cup, he went on checking figures, adding some. Letitia drank her own tea and ate one of the melt-in-the-mouth pastries from a plate, thinking they tasted like Rosa's cooking.

Finished, she took the cups, found the breakfast dishes piled anyhow on the bench, ran hot water over them and stacked the dishwasher. She went to leave then, but asked of the downbent head, 'What time do you want me to be ready, Dominic? It's after five now.'

He glanced up, pen in hand, his interest on other things, then abruptly he smiled at her—fully. 'I like your hair,' he told her. And, funnily, those four words did bring a rush of colour to stain her cheeks.

Observing it, Dominic looked down again, but he

said, 'I think out here by six-thirty, and we'll have our pre-dinner drink all to ourselves. I should have this stuff finished by then.' His hand swung out above all the papers in a throwaway gesture.

Letitia went out, collected her parcels, and while doing so, saw another large box on a chair. It too had a name scrawled right across, but it wasn't a familiar one.

In what she was now coming to think of as her own room, she shook out her new dress from its tissue paper and hung it up. It might not be what Dominic called a pretty dress, but the patterned deep blues and greens reminded her of the fantastically beautiful shallows around Green Island. A low scooped neckline made it a dress to dine in, while the roomy elbow-length magyar sleeves which were a part of the bodice itself provided warmth.

Unwrapping her other packages, she set the make-up on the dressing table, and reflected in the mirror was the neatly folded pair of maroon pyjamas, making her wonder if she would be sleeping here tonight. Then she muttered to herself astringently, 'Of course I'll be here.' Even if Dominic hadn't answered her unspoken question he wouldn't let her go to a motel.

So, taking up one of the new bottles, she marched into the bathroom to set the taps running into the tub. Hadn't she already said once than when in Rome do as the Romans do? She emptied a more than generous portion of bath oil into the swirling water.

And later, exactly on the dot of six-thirty, she gave a last glance at herself. The blue-green patterned dress, drawn in at the waist, hung in silken crêpe de Chine folds to mid-calf, the iridescent colours giving a deeper, darker shade to her eyes. Oh yes, she was satisfied. Her hair was as it should be—hadn't

Dominic said so?

She picked up her small purse and walking to the door, flicked out the light and went out to meet whatever the evening had in store.

She hadn't made any noise, but a voice said, 'In here, Letitia, I'm just fetching the drinks.'

Before she could move towards the kitchen, however, Dominic had emerged. He was carrying a dark green gold-foiled bottle, and some crystal glasses. He stopped, and across the few yards, they looked at one another.

Letitia might have been pleased with her own appearance, but Dominic . . . It wasn't fair, she thought as she had done more than once before. In dark, narrow trousers, with the white tuxedo and black bow-tie, he was as she remembered him from the farmers' dinner; someone, something from out of history's pages. Why, she wondered, was he interested in her? He could have his pick of the beautiful women of the world.

Carefully he was setting down his burden. He came across to her and, taking a hand, raised it to his lips. Merely brushing it, he was saying softly, 'I'm afraid this one gesture is all I can allow myself at this moment. You look beautiful, Letitia.'

'I don't really, Dominic. I've used a lot of make-up, and the dress suits my colouring. But you've been to, and lived in, a great many places in the world. You would know I'm not beautiful.'

Dominic laughed, the sound echoing with deep amusement. 'Didn't you look in your mirror before you came out?'

Letitia nodded. She smiled radiantly at him and said, 'I'll believe that just for tonight. Thank you, Dominic.'

'Good heavens!' He shook his head and busied himself opening the bottle he had brought out. He did it expertly, and she saw the wine froth into the glasses without a drop spilt. He raised his own to her, saying, 'To a wonderful night, Letitia. May we both enjoy it.'

Drinking the cold, tingling liquid, she found she was enjoying it already.

Her companion must have been watching. 'You like it?' he asked. 'I do too. I know champage isn't considered a man's drink, but it's mine.'

Here, abruptly, that pirate's look made the vividly green eyes sparkle as he added, 'Though I do admit that for policy's sake I was drinking spirits on Saturday and Sunday. Hence the need for lots of black coffee when I acquired an unexpected guest.'

Letitia sipped her wine and moved back to sit on a corner of the couch, wishing Dominic wouldn't look at her as he was doing. Breathlessly, she asked, 'Where are we going, did you say?'

At her question, his smile grew deeper. 'We're going to a place called the Northern Heritage. I picked it because I thought it was your sort of place . . .'

He broke off, astonishment taking over his expression, then another look—anger, ruthlessness— surfaced. Someone was knocking at the door. He let it go on for a minute, then moved to open it.

'And to what,' asked a silken voice that held no welcome in it at all, 'do I owe the pleasure of this visit?'

'I wanted to see you, Dominic. I've been trying to get hold of you all day.'

'And if you couldn't, shouldn't that have told you something?'

Heavens! thought Letitia, if he used those words, in that tone, to me, I'd either throw something at him, or walk away!

'Oh, I know what you're like, Dominic. But I wanted to see you. I came around this morning! I didn't think you'd be out, after being up all the night.'

'I wasn't, I was in bed—where you should have been.' Perforce, Dominic moved away from the door, as the woman moved over the threshold.

'Well, I wanted to go check on Joe.'

'And I wonder what the hospital had to say about that?' The words came in the coldest of clipped tones.

The woman, who had her back to Letitia, threw out a dismissing hand, saying, 'The thing is, Dominic, Joe was worried about that girl he brought down here . . .'

'Why in the world would he be worried about her? He knew she'd left with me.'

'I know, but when I rang that motel to see if she was all right they could give me no information at all about her.'

'My dear aunt, motels never give information about their guests.'

Letitia wished Dominic would stop this and let his aunt know she was there. However, he was saying, 'And you wonder, Aunt Jean, why I have this place arranged so no one can get at me! But still, as you *are* here, you might as well have a drink.'

He reached for another glass and filled it with the sparkling, bubbly liquid. 'And you might as well,' he added in the same tone, 'meet my fiancée. We're having our first drink to celebrate. Here, Letitia.' And he smiled an ironical smile across at her.

She had been wondering what she would say to Joe's mother, and the essence of Dominic's words passed over her for a moment.

She had read of it, she believed it just a phrase, but she now she knew it could happen. Because her glass fell, dropped from suddenly nerveless fingers which had no power to hold it. The meaning of his words had penetrated.

'Oops . . . watch your dress!' said Dominic, bending quickly to catch the falling glass. He retrieved it as it reached the carpet.

The glass had not fallen from the other woman's hand, but now she put it to her lips and drank champagne as it was not meant to be drunk.

'You did say . . .' she gasped at Dominic.

'My dear Aunt Jean, I've never suspected that being hard of hearing was a malady you suffered from. Still, as the saying goes, we live and learn.'

Violently angry with Dominic, Letitia spoke. 'I'm sorry . . . yes, I'm the girl Joe took to the football. But I've known Dominic for a long . . .' She stopped. She hadn't known him for a long time.

Then the woman smiled at her and said, 'Don't worry about my nephew here, we're all used to him. She turned to the said nephew. 'I suppose it's really true. You might say such a thing in one of your moods to any of us—but not, however, with the girl present.'

She up-ended the glass, finished the wine, and walked over to the man watching her with an ironical smile on his lips, reaching up to kiss his cheek. 'I'm so pleased,' she said.

'Yes, I imagined you might be.' Cool, unruffled, his reply came, but he was looking over at Letitia.

She knew she was shaking. But Dominic had had no right to come out with something like that as he had done. Whatever she had thought, whatever she might have wanted, she had never allowed herself to hope for this. And he had said so many times that he wanted her. Never that he loved her!

Then he was strolling over to the other side of the lounge, and almost immediately she felt his presence behind her. She felt the warmth of a covering drop about her, then she was pulled back into the circle of Dominic's arms. She felt the shaking begin to stop.

'I made a bet with myself,' he was saying to the room at large, 'that you'd forget to buy something to keep yourself warm. And I won!'

Letitia glanced down; a stole was around her shoulders, a creamy affair as soft as lambswool, woven with silken inlays. It was exquisite. She put her fingers over the hand resting on her waist. It turned, and with dark fingers entwined with her own pale apricot ones, Dominic said, 'Look, I have a table booked. I don't want it to be a late night, so we'll go down with you, Aunt Jean.'

Out on the landing, Letitia heard the door close behind them, and Dominic was at her back as she followed Joe's mother downstairs. He saw his aunt off, then opened the Jaguar's door for Letitia.

'Before you say anything,' he interrupted her, as she went to speak, 'I really didn't mean my proposal to come out of the blue like it did. I intended for us to be encircled by soft lights, sweet music, and glamorous surroundings. But, as with everything else that's happened where we're concerned . . .'

Now, Letitia did interrupt him. She said, 'I'm not

hard of hearing either, Dominic. But did you mean it . . .? Do you really want to . . .?'

Suddenly, impatience and seriousness had gone with the wind. Dominic's dark face, reflected in the dashboard lights, wore only amusement. 'I don't think there are any such things as shotgun marriages nowadays, my love. And even if there were, I can't imagine anyone holding a pistol at my head!'

Neither could Letitia. Her hand went out to him, and was taken in a strong, firm grip. Dominic said, 'Look, I think we'll finish this off where it was intended to start—the restaurant. But first, do I have to wait for my answer?'

He didn't get a smile in return; he got a grin. 'Wouldn't you just get a shock if I said no?' she said.

'Yes, I would indeed get a shock, after what we've been through together. Still, whatever answer you gave would make no difference. One way or another, you'll belong to me!'

'Dominic!' gasped Letitia, almost frightened by the harshness of his words.

Dominic straightened up, drawing in a deep breath, and even from where she sat, Letitia saw the rise and fall of his chest under the white dinner-jacket.

'Sorry,' he said. 'Well, here we go.' And with a jerk she had never before experienced when riding in this car, the Jaguar raced towards the ramp. Letitia sat in her corner seat thinking that some of her companion's remarks had been right. Very few of their encounters had gone smoothly. They had seemed to get off on the wrong foot.

Still, that was all over now. They were going to this restaurant called the Northern Heritage which Dominic had said he had picked because he thought they would suit one another. And in just a few minutes they were passing before an old-fashioned colonial house. Then, with the car parked, Dominic was handing her up veranda steps and into brightly lit space.

She turned a delighted gaze on her companion. They could have walked into a hill station up in the Indian highlands, she thought. It was like a film set. There was not a sign of chromium or modern glass. There were high-backed cane chairs; there were men clad in mess jackets and scarlet cummerbunds hurrying about. But these swiftly moving men were not going about their regiment's business—they were waiting on the guests.

At their table, Dominic glanced at Letitia across the barrier of a large menu, and with relief she saw that everything was back to normal again; that that frightening tone he had used in the car just now was a thing of the past. He was only smiling pleasantly as he enquired, 'Do you like seafood, Letitia?'

The words transported her to another occasion, where Joe had asked the same thing. She answered now, as before, 'Oh, yes, I love seafood. I like almost all food.'

'OK then, seafood first. Then duckling, I think,' he added to the hovering waiter. 'Duckling isn't one of Rosa's best efforts.'

Letitia laughed, and ate what was put before her, gazing around this lovely place. They drank champagne. Dominic raised his glass to her, saying, 'To fewer interruptions, and more time to ourselves. And to you, my love.'

'You've never used an endearment to me before . . . at least not in English.'

'Oh, there was a reason, but we'll go into that later. Now, come and dance with me.'

In his arms, so close, she danced to the soft music

Dominic had mentioned. In his arms she felt again that electricity enfolding their two circling figures. And it was in his arms, thinking of nothing except being where she was, that she was swung suddenly away, and her partner was saying, 'That's enough. We'll finish our dinner, then we'll go.'

Startled, Letitia glanced quickly at his face. She had loved that dancing; she loved the restaurant. What had happened? But as they threaded their way back through the crowded tables, Dominic presented only that handsome, assured appearance she had come to associate with him.

He was waved to and smiled at more than once. He waved and smiled back charmingly, then very definitely gave his attention to his own table. He refused more wine with a few words which earned him a wry smile and a nod of sympathy.

'I explained that I was driving,' said Dominic, then raised a finger, calling for the bill.

'I would have liked to have danced some more,' remarked Letitia ruefully.

'I know. But there'll be plenty of other times. For now . . .' The bill was paid and she found herself walking towards the entrance, wishing she could have stayed in this beautiful place a little longer.

Dominic checked that her dress was free before closing the door and then sliding beneath the wheel in that certain way she was becoming familiar with. He said, 'Fast or slow, Letitia? But I expect tonight it had better be in between.'

Puzzled for a moment, she noticed they were on the familiar route to the range-road. 'Are we going home, Dominic?' she questioned, astonished. 'I've left all my things behind.'

'They won't go astray; no one else is going to be

using that room. And yes, we're going up to
Mareeba. I did intend you to stay at my place, but I
couldn't take another night alone with you, as things
are. But I intend to work them out before we part
tonight. Leave it for now, though, will you,
carissima?'

Oh yes, she would leave anything when he called
her that. She did know some words in Italian. And
she vowed, while watching the countryside flashing
past, that she would take a course in the Italian
lauguage.

She also wondered at what speed Dominic
normally travelled, if this was what he called in
between. The world outside was flying past, and in
the swiftest drive up from Cairns she had ever
participated in, she saw that her driver was easing
the big Jaguar into her own driveway before flicking
out the lights.

'Now,' he said, and with an arm tight about her,
pulled her to him. His kiss when it came was softly
moving, gentle on her mouth. But as it travelled
slowly down the exposed throat, a hand moved to
ease aside the neckline of her dress. There, from one
side to the other, his desire-laden caresses brought
her arching to meet him, and his arm around her
tightened, tightened!

Then a ragged sigh echoed in the confines of the
car, and he said, amusement underlying the tension,
'I don't expect I'd be forgiven if I ripped the top of
this dress as I've done with other garments of yours.
But I would like to, I promise you, and then carry you
home to my place.'

Unable to prevent herself, Letitia asked, 'Then why
not take me home? You have reason to know how I
feel about you.'

'Indeed I have!' Dominic's hand was moving
caressingly across her throat, the rounded breasts,
the drawn-in waist, then downwards over silk-clad

thighs, before slowly returning. Again he sighed, his chest rising sharply. Letitia's fingers, lying against it, felt the tremor.

'Oh yes, I do have reason to know how you feel,' Dominic repeated, and his voice held that strange, slurred tone which she remembered from his apartment. 'But you, Letitia, you can only guess at the way I feel about you!'

She heard his words; but words held no meaning now. All she could take in was being in his arms—and the fact that he meant her to be in them.

'I also know,' he was continuing, 'that I've behaved strangely as far as you're concerned. That, wanting you as I did, I found that always rising between us was a mental block—from the night I almost raped you. And I did nearly do that, Letitia. The anger I felt at seeing you in Madison's arms overcame everything else.

'But later, watching you with him, and wondering . . . then getting the whole sorry mess cleared up, I realised there was only one way I wanted you, but that I'd have to go about it very carefully. I want us to be married, Letitia! Have I told you how much I want you?'

'Oh yes, indeed you have! But you've never said how much you love me.'

'Haven't I really? Well, I promise to show you how much. But I'm afraid it won't be until after we're married—mental blocks being the funny things that they are. So for now, my seductive mistress of the night, I'm going to go home to my own lonely bed. But I'll ring you tomorrow when plans have been set in motion.'

He reached right over her to open her door, and for the briefest second his entire weight was on her as it had been on the night he had just spoken of. Then he was out on his own side, walking her round to the back veranda where a light was burning and the sound of a television echoed.

He didn't kiss her; he didn't even take her hand. He just raised his own in a half-salute and, turning, walked back to the car.

CHAPTER FOURTEEN

THE RAYS of a nearly risen sun slanted in through a small glass aperture to dance dazzlingly over walls and ceiling. But they were not still flashes; they moved and slithered around and about as the boat rode at anchor on a shimmering opaline sea.

A glinting ray moved over the sleeping body of a man, leaving his face in shadow, but came to rest on the closed eyelids of the woman.

Turning, Letitia flung up an arm to shade her eyes—and came awake. Immediately she knew where she was, and she turned carefully. They were going home today, a few days early, but work had been mounting up and, returning from a telephone call yesterday, Dominic had told her, 'I'm afraid, Letitia, we'll have to leave in the morning. I'm needed at home. My coffee isn't behaving itself, and Giovanni gets panic-stricken when that happens. He takes bugs in the tobacco in his stride, but when it comes to my coffee . . .'

So they had had a last dinner on shore, a last ride out to this boat, with the little dinghy engine giving its phut-phut as it took them home. Remembering last night, she smiled dreamily at the golden world through the window. Remembering the whole last month, she smiled dreamily.

She had received the call Dominic had mentioned. She had gone into town and signed papers arranging a wedding. Mr Clinton had said to her as he gathered them up, 'Are you happy, Letitia?'

She had only nodded to this man she had known for so long, not looking at Dominic.

He had laughed, saying, 'Why don't you ask *me* if I'm happy?'

'Oh, I know you will be, Dominic. I've known you always only do what you want to do. I remember when you were little and came to church with your grandmother; you always got what you wanted even then.'

'Oh no, I did not, I'll have you know! But I've got what I want now,' he told the minister. And with those definite words, Dominic took her hand and escorted her out.

He said as they reached the footpath, 'I heard you say in there that you'd like a quiet wedding. I don't think that will be possible, because all my family, never mind all my friends, would wonder why. So I'm afraid you'll have to make up your mind to half the district being at it.'

'But how would I ever manage . . .?' Apprehension coloured Letitia's voice.

'Set your mind at rest,' Dominic told her astringently. 'I don't think either of us will have much say one way or another, once my aunt Jean and my aunt Angela put their heads together. Now, are you happy with the day I arranged—in four weeks' time?'

Again, she had only nodded. She had been happy with that. However, she wasn't happy with one other thing. She hardly saw Dominic on his own. He could have been busy, he probably was, but . . .

And then one morning a week or so later, she glanced up from preparing a salad, to see him standing at the kitchen door. He gazed around the room and a lopsided grin curled his lips. 'I seem to remember this place,' he said, and abruptly a wave of scarlet stained Letitia's cheeks.

Of course! He hadn't been here since the night he had ripped her gown and then swung her up to carry her inside. 'Yes,' she replied tartly, 'you should remember it! But is there a special reason for your presence here now? You might have proposed to me, you might be going to marry me, but no one would guess it from the time we spend together.'

'You know the reason for that! I told you that night I asked you to marry me. And in this waiting time it's more valid than ever now. Look,' he wasn't speaking in that cool, crisp and assured tone that he normally used, as he continued, 'I've come to take you to my place to see if there's anything you want changed. If so, we'll throw it out and . . .'

'Don't be silly, Dominic,' Letitia interrupted. 'It's a dream place, you know that. How would I want to change it?'

'You haven't seen the bedrooms,' was the only answer she received.

No, of course she hadn't! She stood looking at him, searching his face for an expression. And suddenly he was smiling at her, that familiar glinting smile she had reason to know.

'I made it in the daytime, Letitia, because if I take you there at night . . .' Dominic left the sentence unfinished. 'Now come on, the car is just outside.' So they went.

He had opened the big solid front door, Letitia noticed, without any key. So this place wasn't kept locked as the one in Cairns was.

She followed the tall figure through on to the kitchen veranda and then across the little cement path she remembered, to the other tiled veranda.

'This is my . . . this will be the main bedroom,' said Dominic.

It was big, lovely, and flooded with sunshine. It had pale ash furniture that was so in contrast to the heavy carved formal stuff of the lounge and dining room. It also included the largest bed she had ever seen. She was tired of being made to blush, she was having to learn to hold her own. She said now, astringently, 'It's lovely. I wouldn't want to change a thing—anything—in it.'

Unexpectedly, she was caught up in his arms. His head came down, and she was being kissed, achingly, completely. She reached up on tiptoe to clasp her hands behind his neck, responding in every way she knew how.

'For goodness' sake!' Dominic muttered breathlessly, moving her away. 'You run risks, Letitia. How long have we got to this wedding of ours that one night, stupidly, I promised myself I'd wait for? So I simply can't lay you on that bed and make love to you all afternoon as I'd like to, now can I?'

'I don't see why not,' Letitia replied. But she knew he wouldn't. She had thought each day before her wedding would pass on leaden feet, but they didn't. They flew.

She went to Cairns with Marge Kelly to the boutique where she had bought the tangerine dress, and ordered her wedding gown; she arranged for Marge's small daughter to be a flower-girl. She was taken down the mountain range to have dinner at the Peterson house. There she asked Irene, Joe's older sister, if her small daughter would be a flowergirl too. They were the only attendants she wanted.

Hearing this, Dominic hit his forehead. 'Have you no sense?' he asked her. 'They've taken over the entire wedding reception, and now you're handing them the ceremony too!' His aunt smiled, and Letitia laughed, thinking, what do I care? I'm getting Dominic. He must have glanced at her then and seen her expression, for he turned abruptly away.

Then at last the long-awaited day arrived. Dressed, with the organza silk spreading about her, Letitia knew she looked as beautiful as she would ever do. Then Johnny was at her bedroom door. He told her, smiling happily, 'I don't mind you leaving, Sis, because I'm giving you to Dominic.'

Yes, that he was! But she also knew that everything wouldn't be all plain sailing. Not with Dominic. Still . . .

Then as she walked up the aisle with the two little flower-girls scattering frangipani petals before her, her glance went to the men waiting. The shorter, blond one, turned . . . and winked. Well, thank goodness, she thought, Joe couldn't see any expression she might have under the lace veil.

'Dearly beloved——' began Mr Clinton. And later Letitia felt Dominic take her hand, repeating the words he was told to. And then they were out in the vestry.

She looked down at the golden band on her finger and, taking off the azure-blue sapphire and diamond ring from her other hand, eased it on alongside it. She glanced up to meet her new husband's eye. He was so obviously remembering, as she was, the night he had given it to her.

She danced the bridal waltz with Dominic. She danced with other men. She listened to speeches; she ate from plates set before her. It was all hazy. At last Dominic said, 'Go and change, Letitia. If we don't get away now, we never will. These celebrations will be going on all afternoon, and all night too, if I'm any judge.

Glancing out over the happy, laughing, dancing crowd, glasses in hand, champagne on tap as if it were soda-water, Letitia thought he could well be right.

Joe drive them down to Cairns. Dominic told him, 'Remember, mate, this is my car, not yours. And I want us both to get there in one piece.'

Joe grinned, then said, 'And speaking of mates, Dominic, I suppose it wouldn't have been a mate of mine who clobbered my car the day I took Letitia to the football?'

Letitia saw her husband look at her and smile, then answer, 'You really didn't think, Joe, that I'd let you go careering down the range with her in that racing car of yours?' He and Joe both burst out laughing.

Then Dominic had turned away from her to gaze out of his own window, so Letitia lay back in her own corner and did the same, trying to send her mind to other things than the ones it kept returning to. She knew they were going on the water, Dominic had told her to pack casual clothes for it.

And now, in this early morning, on that boat which had been waiting for them, she lay quietly and remembered boarding it. Remembered how they had slid smoothly out of the harbour over a gleaming turquoise ocean, and remembered Dominic calling, 'Come and sit with me, Letitia. Don't bother with unpacking.'

So she had come and sat watching. She had said, 'I didn't know sailing was one of your interests, Dominic,' and heard him reply,

'There are a lot of things about me you don't know. But there's plenty of time ahead of us to find out.'

He turned from her then, giving all his attention to bringing the launch round a headland and into a beach that was protected by two arms of land jutting out into the ocean. He lowered the anchor, and stretched.

'Well, now, my love,' he said, 'to other things.' Down in the larger of the two cabins, Letitia shrugged off her pink linen jacket, kicked off her white sandals, and went over to unpack her case. Dominic said, 'Letitia!' and she was swung up and laid on the bed. And as on other occasions, she was imprisoned between two arms set rigidly on either side of her. Then he had twisted, and beside her, his hand came to rest on her throat. His kisses moving over her lips were still gentle, caressing, but different somehow, holding another quality.

His head lifted a little, and so did his hand. It slid down under the thin voile of her blouse to remain there a moment, fingers outspread on her breasts. Then with laughter echoing deep within his throat, outright amusement colouring his words, he said, 'I know it's barely six o'clock. I know it's nearly summer and bright daylight outside. I know I should be getting ready to take you out dining and dancing on this so important day for you. I do know, too, that making love to you at this beginning of our lives should possibly be in other curcumstances but . . .'

Then she was being kissed, her clothes unbuttoned and unzipped without her thinking of it as Dominic began to really make love to her.

His finger-tips trailed along bare satin skin, his lips kissing each stop they made on the way. With deliberation, he was using all his art and expertise to make need and desire unwind and uncurl within her; **and with scorching,** passionate caresses he was

bringing a response that sent the space about her
flying . . . disintegrating.

Once she moved to fit her body more closely into
the one against her. Once she gasped. But the arms
about her didn't slacken; the body holding her only
brought her more completely to him, and from
somewhere in the world, from somewhere she was
floating above it, she heard Dominic's whisper,
saying, 'Forget everything, my love. Just come with
me.'

Then she was flying, up and up, trying to reach for
something, thinking she would die if her reaching
hands let it slip. And there it was!

She went higher and higher, until the brilliant
crescendo about her exploded into a million vivid
fragments. Then, slowly, still without awareness, she
was drifting down, and as the moments passed, she
came to be conscious of where she was, what had
happened.

She couldn't move away, she was still so
tightly clasped in Dominic's arms. And because he
didn't speak, she also remained silent, wondering . . .

'Did I ever tell you I love you, Letitia?' The words
were uttered from against her throat where his head
was resting.

And in a cabin which was now flooded with
evening sunlight, Letitia smiled, saying, 'Not that I
can remember. However, I do remember you telling
me many times that you wanted me.'

'I did!' He twisted and, raising himself a little on an
elbow, looked down at her.

She said, 'Don't, Dominic.'

'Don't what?' he answered, still gazing down.

'Don't look at me like that!' She was almost
frightened of the driving intensity of passion and
desire in his expression.

For a moment longer he stayed where he was. Then he had swung himself off the bed, saying, 'Get into your swimming gear. We'll go into the beach for a swim. But we'd better hurry.'

Sliding into her bikini, Letitia grabbed up a beach-coat and scrambled up the few steps. Dominic was already there in brief swimming trunks, easing a small dinghy into the water. He helped her in, and swung the engine. The sea was smooth, with only a token swell as the waves washed on to a protected beach. But it wasn't a brilliant, scintillating sapphire now; it was turning to dark indigo.

They swam in water that was warm, but not for long. Late evening was shark time. Then, as they strolled along the firm yellow sand, Dominc took her hand. But he was quiet.

'It's lovely, this time of the day, isn't it?' she spoke softly, as if afraid to spoil the hush of evening. Then behind them, lights from dwellings began to come on and the first faint stars shone in a sky turning now from hazy blueness to the dark of a swifly coming night.

Dominic broke his silence, as the beach emptied itself of the last swimmer. 'We'll go too,' he said.

As the little dinghy chugged them back over the now black water to their temporary home, Letitia glanced down at the two bands on her finger, one plain gold, the other glinting in the faint star-shine.

For the next ten days Dominic opened up a new world for her as they cruised a turquoise ocean. They ate on deck, they swam, they dined at tourist hotels, then finally they headed for Port Douglas. Easing into a marina there was different. They stayed at a motel, and Letitia explored while Dominic worked.

She had just showered and was blow-drying her

hair on the second evening, when he arrived
back—late.

He stood with his back against the door and smiled
across at her, and seeing the expression on his face,
she wondered what was coming. She couldn't help
herself saying, however, 'You're all dirty.'

'Indeed I am. And you look like water to a man
dying of thirst in the desert. Dare I come and put my
arms around you?'

Involuntarily she backed off. 'I've never seen you
in that state before,' she told him. 'I didn't think you
actually worked, Dominic!'

'Now, didn't you? Well, allow me to inform you
that there's work and work, and mine is a lot harder
than the physical kind. But today, some bother had to
be straightened out. It's now been done.

'However, I was going to ask if you'd mind very
much eating here in the restaurant by yourself,
because . . .' here, Dominic began to laugh, that silent
shaking that betokened amusement at something he
thought funny, 'I have to attend a working dinner
with bankers, contractors, unions, the lot. You don't
mind, do you, *carissima*?'

'Of course I don't.'

Letitia didn't finish with an endearment in Italian,
but the glance she sent across to him carried
memories. Dominic had made these last days fly for
her on scented wings, so of course she wouldn't
mind doing any little thing he asked of her . . .
anything!

Out of the shower, he was dressing quickly, and
Letitia watched his reflection in the mirror as he
placed necessities into his pockets. She saw that his
expression was intent, almost severe. So different
from any of those expressions he had ever presented
to her. He turned suddenly and saw her watching.
He raised an eyebrow.

'What is it?' he asked.

'Nothing, I was just finishing my hair.'

'Don't say nothing to me, my inexpert little story-teller! Don't you realise that by now I know every nuance your voice carries?'

'Oh no, you don't!' Her very tone was indignant. 'You might think you do, but you don't.'

Dominic walked across to slide his arms about her back, bringing her to him. 'OK,' he said, 'I don't.' He bent and kissed her, fully, completely, achingly. 'And that,' he interposed, 'is something I shouldn't be doing, if I'm to keep my mind on tonight's affair. Now, can I escort you to the restaurant?'

Letitia shook her head. 'No, I'm going to buy my own dinner. I'm going to that shop I saw to get fish and chips.' She looked at him, daring him to either laugh or say she couldn't.

She saw that for a change his eyes were wide open as they gazed directly at her; that he wasn't going to laugh. Then he said, 'All right, I know the one. You shouldn't get into any trouble there. Come along, I'll see you outside.'

He waved a hand, going on his way, and in the take-away shop Letitia waited her turn for the fish and chips, remembering how often she and Johnny had done this same thing. Then she strolled back to the motel. She was asleep when Dominic returned.

But now a voice speaking so close beside her made her jump and she turned, startled. She said, 'I thought you were still asleep, Dominic. You were lying there so quietly.'

'Oh, I was trying to work out what I'd do first—get up, have my wife bring me breakfast in bed, or stay here in this paradise and let my coffee plantation go hang, or even . . .' His voice changed, and she had come to know that tone.

'Or even,' he repeated, 'begin on something much more to my taste. Because if we have to go, I'm entitled to indulge myself a little before we do.' He reached out to take her in his arms.

Letitia put a hand against the bare, smooth chest, to fend him off.

Dominic drew back immediately, but his eyebrow rose, and she said quickly before he could move or speak, 'Dominic, about going home . . . Things will be different, you know. They'll have to be. And I've seen how you don't like to be bothered, harassed. Up at the farm maybe, it shouldn't matter so much, but in Cairns. And also . . .'

Her voice trailed away because she couldn't imagine Dominic, so assured, so immaculate, with that aura of charisma which was an integral part of him, being involved in an ordinary domestic day-to-day living.

But he was laughing at her—not silently, either, but with a low chuckle of amusement that echoed around the small sunlit cabin.

'I don't see what's so funny,' she told him tartly. 'You know what I mean—you know you do. So you can stop laughing.' She went to spring out of the bed, but his arm, quicker than she was, brought her back.

'Look, Letitia,' he said, his laughter disappearing, his demeanour turning serious, 'I admit that up till now I *have* guarded my privacy. But that was from my family. I would never have had a private life if I hadn't done so . . .' He paused before continuing. 'Then one day I went with Giovanni to pay my respects to a neighbouring young girl and boy, whose grandfather both my father and I had known . . . and I met you!'

He was lying flat beside her now, arms crossed

over his head. Glancing sideways, Letitia saw that a frown had come to gather between his brows. Then he was continuing, 'Look, I'm not trying to say the earth fell in on top of me at that moment. But I did find myself inventing an excuse to go along to your place that evening—something, I might tell you, that I'd never done, or had reason to do, before.

'And later on—I couldn't believe it! I'd travelled the world, and of course I've had my . . . liaisons. After all, I'm nearly thirty years old, and to find I was suddenly head over heels in love was hard for me to believe. But there it was! And even though I found you showed a . . . liking for me, I would have moved heaven and earth to get you if you hadn't. So . . . do those few words answer your question about our going home? If they don't, I will also add that being harassed in the way I hope to be is all I'm going to ask of life from now on. So is there anything else, because I think you interrupted a more enjoyable subject?'

'Is it enjoyable, Dominic?' Letitia questioned softly when she was once more in his arms. All she got for a reply was a low laugh, different entirely from the one he gave when amused. But if he wasn't answering; if he wasn't talking; he was showing her in other ways how enjoyable it could be.

She lay there, silver-gilt hair cascading over a bare brown arm; she lay there, grey eyes hazed with the passion and desire he was generating. Then they were fused together, and there was nothing left but heights to climb. Over entwined limbs of pale apricot, the darkness of gleaming bronze, the early sun-rays ran shimmering. And later, in the small sunlit cabin, only stillness registered, only silence echoed.

Then as the moments passed, Dominic came up on one elbow. He said, 'Do I apologise for things maybe getting a little out of control just now? Are you all right?' This was Dominic, the assured, the arrogant, speaking carefully.

So she smiled and answered in a voice still not entirely her own, 'I expect they might have a little. Do you think you could be blamed for that?'

The backs of his fingers stroking down her cheeks, he said, 'Oh, no, I hold you wholly responsible. But did I ever tell you I love you, Letitia?'

'Oh, I think somewhere along the line I have a memory of hearing you say so,' she replied, her tone back to normal again.

'OK then, stay there while I put the kettle on, then we'll head for home . . . and for anything else the gods may see fit to provide.' He bent over to kiss her and said something in Italian, then was gone before she could ask for a translation.

But Letitia didn't stay in bed. She showered lavishly with the only commodity which had been in short supply on this trip, because fresh water couldn't be carried in quantity . . . but now they were going home. Then, dried, she donned citrine shorts and top and a yellow headband across her forehead. It would be needed outside in the breeze.

Dominic came to the cabin doorway, saying, 'Tea's up.' His glance ran over her from head to foot, and he said, grinning, 'Did I ever tell you you're beautiful?'

She answered, being able now to take his remarks —or some of them—with composure, 'I do remember you saying something like that along the line—and that I didn't believe you.'

He laughed, saying, 'Come and have some tea and toast. We'll eat properly when we get home.'

The small meal finished, they went topside. Dominic reached out an arm to bring Letitia to him. So they stood, with the wind streaming past, and a vast, scintillating lapis-lazuli ocean about them.

Then, faintly on the horizon, a hazy smudge of land appeared, coming ever clearer as the launch slid the miles behind them. It was Cairns and home . . . and, as Dominic had said, whatever else the gods decided to provide.

Coming Next Month

#3031 THE ASKING PRICE Amanda Browning
Sian wants to leave the past behind, but Blair Desmond, her attractive new boss, blames her for the death of his friend. He is wrong, of course, but even if he'd listen to her explanations, would he believe her?

#3032 RED HOT PEPPER Roz Denny
Take a stubborn redhead named Pepper Rivera and a rakish but charming major named Dev Wade. Add two matchmaking fathers, five overprotective brothers, one flashy sports car and an overgrown sheepdog. Then wait for the sparks—and the fur—to fly.

#3033 WHEN WE'RE ALONE Jane Donnelly
Corbin is a persistent investigative reporter, and Livvy finds it hard not to fall under his spell. The more involved they become, the harder it is to keep any secrets from him. And there's one secret he simply must never discover. . . .

#3034 ISLAND DECEPTION Elizabeth Duke
Gemma's relaxing holiday on the Great Barrier Reef while getting over her broken engagement is spoiled by her clashes with resident doctor Chad Rivers—who thinks Gemma is an empty-headed model. And Gemma isn't about to tell him that she is a doctor, too.

#3035 QUEEN OF HEARTS Melissa Forsythe
On her way to Nice to play in an international bridge tournament Nikki Damon learns that you can't bring a fantasy to life—in her case, by kissing a handsome stranger in Paris—and expect to walk away, as if it never happened.

#3036 NO NEED TO SAY GOODBYE Betty Neels
If Louise ever thinks about Dr. Aldo van der Linden, it is as a professional colleague, not as a man. Until the day he involves himself in the affairs of her family, particularly her sister Zoe. Somehow, Louise finds it difficult to be pleased.

Available in February wherever paperback books are sold, or through Harlequin Reader Service:

In the U.S.
901 Fuhrmann Blvd.
P.O. Box 1397
Buffalo, N.Y. 14240-1397

In Canada
P.O. Box 603
Fort Erie, Ontario
L2A 5X3

A compelling novel of deadly revenge and passion
from Harlequin's bestselling international
romance author Penny Jordan

POWER PLAY

Eleven years had passed but the
terror of that night was something
Pepper Minesse would never
forget. Fueled by revenge against
the four men who had brutally
shattered her past, she set in
motion a deadly plan to destroy
their futures.

Available in February!

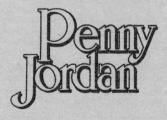

 Harlequin Books ®

HPP-1A

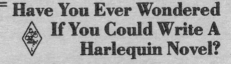

Have You Ever Wondered If You Could Write A Harlequin Novel?

Here's great news—Harlequin is offering a series of cassette tapes to help you do just that. Written by Harlequin editors, these tapes give practical advice on how to make your characters—and your story—come alive. There's a tape for each contemporary romance series Harlequin publishes.

Mail order only

All sales final

Harlequin Superromance®

LET THE GOOD TIMES ROLL...

Add some Cajun spice to liven up your New Year's celebrations and join Superromance for a romantic tour of the rich Acadian marshlands and the legendary Louisiana bayous.

Starting in January 1990, we're launching CAJUN MELODIES, a three-book tribute to the fun-loving people who've enriched America by introducing us to crawfish étouffé and gumbo, zydeco music and the Saturday night party, the *fais-dodo*. And learn about loving, Cajun-style, as you meet the tall, dark, handsome men who win their ladies' hearts with a beautiful, haunting melody....

Book One: *Julianne's Song*, January 1990
Book Two: *Catherine's Song*, February 1990
Book Three: *Jessica's Song*, March 1990

Step into a world of pulsing adventure, gripping emotion and lush sensuality with these evocative love stories penned by today's bestselling authors in the highest romantic tradition. Pursuing their passionate dreams against a backdrop of the past's most colorful and dramatic moments, our vibrant heroines and dashing heroes will make history come alive for you.

Watch for new Harlequin Historicals each month, available wherever Harlequin Books are sold.

History has never been so romantic!